THE WORST VILLAIN EVER

THE WORST VILLAIN EVER

AMY BEARCE

Turner, OR

J
Bearce

THE WORST VILLAIN EVER
Copyright © 2022 by **Amy Bearce**
www.amybearce.com

Published by Snowy Wings Publishing
www.snowywingspublishing.com
PO Box 1035, Turner, OR 97392

First Edition:
ISBN   978-1-952667-78-7 (ebook)
ISBN   978-1-952667-79-4 (paperback)

Cover layout and typography by Qamber Designs and Qamber Kids
Cover illustration by Oh Lenic
Interior Formatting by Qamber Designs

To my earliest readers

Thanks for cheering me on for all these years!

CHAPTER 1

THE LETTER

GEORGE PRUWELL PEERED out from his second-story window, wearing his Mastermind Magnifying Goggles. With those bad boys on, he could see the yellow centers of Mrs. Wutherford's daisies all the way across the street. But George was far less interested in the daisies than in what would hopefully be his first successful villainous trick.

He zeroed in on the sidewalk and saw nothing. Excellent. He'd hidden the Trip 'Em Stakes on either side of the cement and made sure the wire stretching between them was invisible. He'd perfected an invisible tripwire using Gloss Over-It[1] to make sure he followed rule number

---

1   Gloss-Over-It: Sold at The Thrifty Villain store and website for only $9.99. The product description reads, "A unique blend of chemicals that refract light to make small objects almost unnoticeable. A priceless addition for villains who must pay attention to prices."

one of high villainy: Don't get caught.

The thought of someone tripping and landing in a glorious spill of flailing limbs and scattered papers should have made George smile with anticipation. Any self-respecting villain would be rubbing his hands together in glee. Perhaps even cackling maniacally. Instead, George felt like he had swallowed a dozen white mice from a mad scientist's laboratory.

Chewing a thumbnail, he turned his gaze north. Mike Jones was coasting down the sidewalk on his skateboard, as he did every evening. George seriously wished someone else had been a handier victim, but Mike passed this spot like clockwork. Mike always waved at George when they saw each other, even though they had never actually spoken.

George squirmed. Maybe he should just hit the *terminate* button on his handmade Tripwire Remote. It would wind up the tripwire into one of the hidden Trip 'Em Stakes, clearing the sidewalk in seconds. He could always try tomorrow.

But it would be the third cancelled trick this week, and he so wanted to see one of his tricks finally work. He *needed* one to work.

Mike's black skateboard had giant red wheels that flashed as they spun. It was a sweet board, especially for a Regular Public Citizen, or "RPC," as they were known among villains. George's skateboard was better, with jets in the back for quick escapes if—*no, when!*—he became a villain-in-training. He was sure his acceptance letter from the Academy of Villainy and Wrongdoing would come any day now—he was eleven, for villainy's sake—but landing at least one solid trick would make him feel better about his odds.

As Mike approached the tripwire, George leaned forward.

Everything looked perfect—so perfect, in fact, that George broke out in a sweat. Mike really might go flying when his skateboard came to a sudden and complete stop.

Oh man, George thought. *I hope he doesn't get hurt!* Mike wasn't a bad guy, after all.

Technically, that was George's job—being a bad guy. He wasn't very good at it. No doubt Alex, his big brother, would have found a way to not only successfully trip Mike, but to pick his pockets while he was flying through the air. *Alex* wouldn't be feeling anxious right now.

Pressing the magnifying button next to his left eye, George zeroed in closer. Mike was singing along to some song, earbuds barely visible through his hair. Pulling back on the zoom, George counted down as Mike approached the trap.

As he got closer and closer, George's finger hovered over the *terminate* button.

Mike was almost there. He would hit the wire for sure.

With a huff, George pressed the button to stop the trick and then sagged against the window. He'd chickened out. *Again.*

But the red light on the remote didn't flash. The wire wasn't moving. *Oh no...*

Jerking back to his feet, he smacked the goggles to his face and forced himself to watch, grimacing in anticipation.

But right as Mike was about to cross the trap, a man in a black ski mask burst out from Mrs. Wutherford's house, carrying a laptop. He was running full-out with Mrs. Wutherford screaming behind him, "Stop! Thief!"

Mike screeched his board to a halt, and the thief bolted in front of him. The thief hit the hidden wire and went sailing through the air before falling on his face. The laptop went flying harmlessly into the grass. George smacked his hand against his forehead.

Mrs. Wutherford kept the masked man on the ground by hitting him repeatedly with her watering can, and Mike was calling someone on his phone—probably the police.

The police!

George hit the *retract* button again and again. The police would no doubt be here in a heartbeat. No matter what, they could not find that tripwire. *Remember rule number one!* If the button didn't work, he'd have to find some excuse to run out there, and he was terrible at lying.

A patrol car pulled up. George squeaked, "Come on! Come on!" He hit the remote on the table.

The remote's red light suddenly lit up, and he let out a long whoosh of air. His secret was safe. The red light meant the wire had spooled into the hidden casing. Both stakes were safely hidden under the leaves. He'd collect his trap later, when the coast was clear.

George was caught between deepest relief and hugest despair. When the police car arrived, two officers stepped out: a big guy and a woman with mirrored sunglasses. Fumbling in his rush, George jammed on his Eavesdropping Ears and aimed his amplifier toward Mike and the police officers. The big guy spoke first.

"What's going on here, young man?"

"Dude, that guy just came running out of the house, and like, tripped on the sidewalk or something."

"Is anyone hurt?"

The police officers and Mike looked over at the slouching burglar being cuffed by the cop's partner. Mrs. Wutherford seemed to be shouting words that not even criminals should hear.

Mike laughed. *"Maybe just the crook."*

"Thank you for your time, then."

George sighed with relief. No one even looked near his trap device. That was good news. But the only other thing he could be thankful for was that his family would never know he had yet another failure in his villainy résumé.

Not only had he *not* taken down a good guy, he'd accidentally taken down a bad guy! Talk about horrible luck. And even worse, if he were honest with himself, George had to admit he was *glad* Mike was safe and Mrs. Wutherford had gotten her laptop back. If he found out, Alex would never, *ever* let him live that one down.

Well, next time, George would build an even *better* trap. And no matter how bad he might feel when it worked, he'd tough it out. He had sworn long ago to honor

• 6 •

the family name. It was the one thing his mother had ever asked of him and his brother. And it was the least George could do for his dad.

George laid aside his goggles, grabbed his backpack, and trudged downstairs to collect his messed-up trap. "A good villain never wastes anything," his dad used to say. Of course, now his dad just sent letters with advice through the high-security prison mail system. If the locks at that joint had been mechanical, his dad would have broken out years ago, but computerized locks required a whole different type of expertise. People had to specialize these days.

The red-and-blue lights had faded away. The street looked the same as always, a row of manicured lawns and two-story clapboard houses. No one would ever suspect a villain family lived here, which was the whole point, of course. They had to stay under the radar of RPCs.

George slipped out the front door of his house. As he crossed the street, he hung his head for a moment before jerking his chin up. Alex could be watching. In fact, he might have watched the whole crime fumble and seen the mortifying capture of a crook. Now that Alex was back from the Academy, their mother couldn't stop talking about how proud she was of him, graduating top in his class. Like father, like son. But unlike the father, Alex had never been caught—and probably never would be.

Now a proud and professional villain, Alex had done a lot to save their family name, even as a student. He'd probably earn his Distinguished Villain plaque before George even graduated. That award would place Alex on the wall of fame in the Great Villain Council building, where rows and rows of Pruwell names, generations of George's ancestors, shined among the golden plaques. Well, except their father's. But at least he'd had a plaque and a brilliant career as a safecracker—until he'd gotten busted. George might not ever get started. But he so wanted to make his family proud.

Alex's triumphant return made George more desperate than ever to show he could be villain material too. How could two brothers be so different?

Alex was as broad-shouldered as George was scrawny. His stylish dark hair stayed perfectly in place, but George's brown curls corkscrewed wildly. And every day, Alex asked with a sneer, "Any mail, little bro?" forcing George to admit, yet again, that no letter had come. It almost made him jealous of RPCs, who at least had no idea they were missing out on a whole other world of villainy and intrigue.

Pausing on the sidewalk, George casually scanned

the area, trying to look as if everything had gone according to plan. He yanked up the Trip 'Em Stakes. At least the trap had been practically invisible. The thief had proven that. George wasn't a *total* failure.

Just as he finished tucking the stakes into the backpack, the mail truck pulled up to George's house. The jaunty white mail truck always made his heart beat faster. Usually, the only things delivered were coupons for PizzaRama, computer magazines for Alex, and what his mother called "endless bills." But today could be different.

George thought that every day, though, and so far, nothing had changed.

The mailman stuffed something into their box. Something small. As soon as the truck drove off, George ran over to the mailbox, heart crammed tightly in his throat. He wished he had a good luck charm to hold on to.

He took a deep breath and yanked opened the little door. A single letter waited. A black letter with a gold seal.

George's heart raced faster than a baddie escaping a con job. Pulling out the letter with shaking hands, he forced himself to look at the return address. It was from *them*. And it was addressed to George Pruwell.

CHAPTER 2

THE NEWS

WOWSERS! KNEES WEAK, George tucked the letter under his arm and raced up the stairs to his room. His DO NOT ENTER: EVIL AT WORK sign swayed wildly on the hook as he slammed the door and tossed his bag under his bed.

Barely breathing, George ripped open the envelope.

Greetings from the prestigious and infamous Academy of Villainy and Wrongdoing. You are invited to audition for an exclusive spot in our villain trainee program during the Academy's annual Trial Week. Students who successfully complete Trial Week will join the school as a villain trainee.

George let out a wild yell. He stomped around his room, accidentally breaking two of his favorite villain action figures in his excitement. *Wait till Alex gets a load of* this!

George ran past their mom's sewing room and

flung open Alex's door. The room was pitch-black, but that was not uncommon.

"I got the letter, Alex! I got it!"

Silence was the only answer. George squinted into the darkness and took one step inside. "Alex?"

"Perhaps you've forgotten the rules, little brother. Try. Again." Alex's voice was soft but rippling with threat. The slight growl added to the endearment made George shiver. How could he have forgotten the rule, even now?

Stepping into Alex's room always required special permission. Lowly little brothers did not just bust into the room of Alexander the Terrible, the highest-scoring member of the villain trainee program of his graduating year. Alex had managed to rob the most secure bank in the city as his capstone project last spring, at only sixteen years of age. Such an advanced achievement placed Alex as someone firmly dedicated to their family's long tradition of high villainy. From that point on, Alex had required George to call him "Alexander the Terrible, the Best Villain of our Time."

George shuffled his feet, wanting to shout out the excellent news, but common sense and plenty of experience with his brother's moods convinced him to back out of the room and close the door. He cleared his throat, knocked, and counted to ten to help squash the fear that always swamped him when he spoke to his brother.

"You may enter." His brother's command was deep, echoing, rolling. Alex hadn't even needed to take Intimidating Voices 101. He was a natural.

George opened the door. A light flared, faintly red, and a candle flickered in the corner. Alex took the instruction to have an evil lair quite seriously, though he couldn't afford his own cave or skyscraper yet. He said he was working on his next big scheme, though he mostly seemed to be working at improving his video game skills.

The shape of his brother's shadow, leaning back in his easy chair, took form against the wall. Alex stared at him, eyes dark and unreadable.

"Now what was so important that you had to breach protocol?" Alex asked, boredom seeping through every word.

George had to clear this throat again. "I... I got invited to try out. For the Academy."

More silence. He shifted his feet and waited for a response, chewing on his fingernails.

"Well, I *am* your brother," Alex finally replied. "Lucky for you, that makes up for your... deficiencies. They'll all assume you'll turn out like me."

George felt like a balloon just popped by a needle.

They both knew what Alex meant. Their parents had never worried about Alex's career. Just George's. Right before Dad had been taken away to the clink, he'd knelt in front of seven-year-old George and made him solemnly promise to do his best to be a villain. Villainy was part of him, Dad had said, even when it didn't feel easy. No one ever needed to remind Alex what he was supposed to be. No one ever doubted he'd make it big.

George shoved the letter in his back pocket. "Yeah, I guess."

Alex's voice grew sharper. "*Yeah*?"

"Yes," George corrected quickly and stood straighter.

"Yes, what?" Alex said.

"Yes, Alexander the Terrible, the Best Villain of Our Time."

"I'll be amazed if you don't flunk out first thing, but try not to, okay, little bro? I'd be totally humiliated." He turned his attention back to his game.

Shame flared along George's cheeks. Alex had a point. Their family had lost enough already. Their dad was the first in their family to lose his plaque and his cushy retirement, the goal of most villains—well, except the mad scientists obsessed with destroying the world.

If George failed to get into the Academy, his dad would also be the first villain in the Pruwell family with a son who didn't get into the school at all. George didn't care about money, but he did care about his dad. The possibility of failing made George feel like he'd fallen through a trapdoor.

His brother smirked, his white teeth gleaming in the darkness. Villains could go for creepy and scary or for slickly handsome. Alex was slick enough to skate on. Tall, dark hair, sharp cheekbones. But he hadn't been able to grow the long, twirling moustache many traditional villains wore, which gave George secret glee.

One day, George would grow himself a big, black mustache and twirl it in front of his brother, after having been dubbed "George the Feared" or maybe even "George, the Worst Villain of Our Time!" Calling a villain the *worst* villain, not the *best*, always made more sense to him. Clearly, since villains were bad already, they'd go from bad to worst.

Alex waved a hand in dismissal, and George wasted no time.

Back on the other side of Alex's firmly shut door, George could finally breathe properly. He examined the letter again, barely skimming the details at the end. The main thing was, they'd invited him!

Maybe he wasn't as villainous as his brother yet, or even his mom, who helped scoundrels find the perfect attire, but he could do this. He was starting behind the curve, but he wouldn't shame his parents. He would prove to them all he was just as much a member of this family as Alex.

CHAPTER 3

THE PREPARATION

GEORGE WAS GOING to rock out at the Academy, but there were so many things to do before leaving! He was due to arrive tomorrow. The last-minute arrival of the invitation was standard. Villains always had to be ready at a moment's notice.

Mom was going to be so proud, of course. Despite Dad's long-term stay in the slammer, she had still determinedly raised her sons to be professional villains. Even when George hadn't shown the expected natural aptitude.

Her eyes had watered with pride when Alex crushed ladybugs with his bare feet when he'd been as young as three. But George had just wanted to keep ladybugs as pets, which horrified her. Poisonous snakes or biting lizards, sure, but not ladybugs, or puppies or—*villainy forbid it*—kittens! Once, he'd found two quarters on the ground and told his mom he'd lifted them from a kid down the block.

She'd given him double dessert that night. But the guilt had nagged at him. When he confessed his lie, his mom sighed and shook her head. She hadn't looked surprised at all.

It wasn't so much that George didn't like doing villainous things. He just felt better when he didn't. But he knew enough not to mention that part.

The garage door creaked open downstairs. He grabbed his letter from his pocket and slid down the banister. He stood in the kitchen and wore a giant grin when his mom walked through the door, holding two bags of groceries.

Her curly red hair was all that could be seen over bunches of green radish tops. George's hair had the same curls but brown like his dad's. She kicked the door closed behind her with a red high heel. Her red dress had what looked like white polka dots but were actually tiny white skulls.

"Let me help you with that, Mom," George said as he hurried to her side.

"Thanks, George. I really shouldn't let you help— bad habits sneak in like little foxes, you know!" She blew a strand of hair out of her face. "But you would not *believe* the day I had at the store! I was the only one at the register all morning, and then Mr. Albatross sent a memo saying we had a meeting at ten, but then he moved it to nine, so everyone was late, and he was *furious*—"

"Mom!"

"And *then* I had to close Ms. Furtively's account because she never paid her bill for the matching archvillain and sidekick outfits[2]—she even got the silver-edged *capes*, for crying out loud. She was so mad! She said I obviously knew nothing about villain fashion and probably wore pink polyester pants at home. I almost asked Alex to make her sorry, but he's got more *important* crimes to commit—"

"Mom!" George shouted.

She paused, mouth open, and he took the momentary—and unusual—silence as his opportunity to wave his letter of invitation under her nose.

"I get to try out," he said into the silence.

She did not need any more information than that. "Oh, my horrible honey!" she cried, giving him a tight hug. She wiped her eyes and sniffed. "My baby is growing up! Eleven already and about to try out at the Academy! I

---

2   From *Villains on the Cutting Edge ... of Fashion*: The Latest Designs in Villain Fashion. View our latest *Him and Her Matching Apparel*, as well as stroll through our *Sidekick Café*, to see the most dastardly duds you can dare to don.

wasn't sure this day would ever come!"

George flushed. "Mom, please."

"No, really! Your father will be so proud. I'm sure that you'll do fantastically horrible deeds and then—*oh!* You and your brother can be an evil duo! There hasn't been one of those in over seventy years, since the Carnage Brothers retired!"

She dropped her grocery bag and clapped again, black-tipped nails flashing. "This calls for a celebration!" she said with a giant smile. "Roasted radishes!"

George didn't even sigh. Radishes, turnips, and other bitter foods were the norm for a villain-in-training. His mother intended to give him every head start, especially given his unfortunate tendencies.

A very unvillainous warmth oozed through George as he thought about how much his mom had sacrificed to give him and his brother every advantage, providing everything they could ask for. And now her dreams were coming true. And his, too, of course.

As soon as he graduated from the Academy, he'd be a real villain at last. His final capstone project would earn him the coveted *Pronouncement of Official Villain Status* certificate from the High Villain Council. He would be granted entrance into secret societies and networking sites for villain resources. He would eventually take advanced classes for criminal mastermind status. He would earn his Distinguished Villain plaque and join the ranks of great villains like Stephen the Owl—so called for his giant spectacles—and Gracie Schnoodlehaven, who'd first figured out that people would pay huge prices for fake brand names if the advertisements were clever enough. Hers always were.

Of course, first he had to audition.

Mom left a coded message with the jail to tell Dad the good news. She even came up with jellied pig feet for dessert in celebration. Then George went upstairs to pack. His mom had already arranged his flight for first thing in the morning.

He folded his shirts and pants and grabbed his favorite books to bring too. *One Hundred and Twelve Villain Tricks* by Alison the Caper-Queen. *Villainy for Life*, a memoir by Sir Grandon Highbrow. His magazine collection of *Villains Quarterly*. And of course, the catalog of *Tools of the Trade: Villains Unstoppable*, full of the newest and coolest tools and gadgets for any kind of villain.

He traced the cover and wondered if life would be

the same there. Would he have time to lie on his bed and dream about ray guns and gadgets? Or would he be busy all the time, doing homework and villainous activities? Assuming he could do them properly.

His arms and legs suddenly felt like the bone marrow in the oxtail Mom cooked on special holidays: gelatinous goo. He shook his head and packed the catalog in the bottom of his new suitcase. He'd spent so much time hoping he'd get into villain school that he'd never really thought much about what would happen next. Well, no matter how hard life was at the Academy, he'd learn.

Time sped by, and soon bedtime loomed. Before he got into his pajamas, though, he needed to talk to Daniel, his one friend despite him being an RPC.

George used to wish he went to a regular elementary school like Daniel. They had neat classes like art and music, and plenty of villain-family kids went to RPC schools and still made it into the Academy. But when he'd briefly attended a normal school alongside RPC kindergarteners, he'd come home with bad habits like sharing and saying please and thank you. His mom had pulled him out of the class. No RPC friends became their family rule.

George's family belonged to a small co-op for

homeschooling villain families from around the city. Their co-op did things like playing tricks on each other, building phone taps, and camouflaging pretend evil lairs. While George enjoyed some of these activities, he didn't like it when the kids were mean to each other, something that was highly encouraged.

He'd regularly had his feet stomped on and been laughed at when he cried. Last year, one kid put numbing gel on the other kids' cups so that when they took a drink, they drooled all over themselves. That kid was already at the Academy, probably top of his class.

George looked over at his letter of invitation on the desk. For the first time, really, he began to wonder if the Academy was going to be as fantastic as he'd always thought. He gulped, then went out to visit his only friend one last time.

George slipped across the yard to Daniel's house, carrying a pillowcase that bulged along the bottom. His real friendship with Daniel had managed to slip by George's mom's RPC radar. George had told her spending time with a non-villain was practice for Deceit 201, by having to keep up a secret identity. She'd been delighted to hear him planning for his future in villainy.

George tapped on his friend's window with their secret knock.

Daniel slid open the pane with a grin, already in pajamas. "Hey, what's up? Want to ride bikes tomorrow?"

George looked around, hoping Alex wasn't spying. Bike riding was not a very villainous activity. "Sorry, I can't. But could you help me with something?"

Now that Daniel was looking at him expectantly, the words stuck in George's throat. He wasn't allowed to tell the truth.

George held up the overstuffed pillowcase. "Well, it's kind of... uh... could you use the seeds and nuts in here to feed the family of squirrels in our front tree while I'm gone for a while?" The words tripped on each other as they sped out of his mouth. "They just had babies a couple months ago when the drought hit, and I wanted to make sure the babies had enough food. But now I think they sort of depend on it."

And their little fluffy tails are really cute.

"Wait, you're going somewhere?" Daniel looked closely at George, who tried not to blink too much or stare too long without blinking. Either one meant lying. Alex lied like he breathed—naturally and with a lot of hot air—but George had to study the art.

"My mom's sending me to a private school, a boarding school, for a couple of years."

"No way! Where? When?"

"Tomorrow. New York," George said. Wait! Could he even say New York? That part was true. Darn it, he should have planned out a speech.

Daniel gaped at him. "Of course I'll feed the squirrels, but that stinks you'll be gone all of a sudden. It won't be the same around here without you."

"I'll text and call and stuff, okay?"

"Sure, okay." Daniel smiled. He was too nice to even pitch a fit about not knowing until the last minute.

George's eyes stung a little. He took a deep breath and handed over the pillowcase.

Daniel swung it over his shoulder. "Wanna come in for some carrots or something?"

It had taken months to teach Daniel and his mom that George really wasn't going to eat the cookies they kept offering. They smelled great, but they were strictly forbidden for a villain. Too much sweetness could ruin a villain's tolerance for bitterness and cynicism. "I can't. I've got to finish packing."

Daniel nodded but added, "Hey, it was nice of you to help out the squirrels. I'm sure you'll make lots of new friends there, George. You're a really good person."

George flinched and took a quick glance up and down the street. "Thanks, Daniel."

He waved at Daniel and fled back home.

When he climbed under his too-stiff bedspread that felt like cardboard (standard for villains-in-training— it kept them cranky), he gave a huge sigh of relief. The squirrels would be fine. And thank villainy no one had heard Daniel call him such a terrible thing. Being marked as a nice person was the last thing he needed right before auditioning at the world's most famous school for villains.

CHAPTER 4

THE BIG DAY

AT 4:00 A.M. the next morning, George's mom was waiting in the car, engine running, ready to get George on his way. His plane would fly nonstop straight from Omaha, Nebraska, to New York City. He had never visited Alex at the Academy. It went against Academy Policy to have family visits[3]. Now it felt like worms were roiling in George's stomach from a strange blend of excitement and nerves.

He opened the car door but turned when Alex unexpectedly strode out of the house. George's brother

---

3   *Academy Student Handbook*, page 14,777: "Note that if *any* family member visits you, at *any* point, even if 'it was just for two minutes to bring me my new life-support system,' you will find your belongings on the side of the road for any wandering vagabond to take. It doesn't take a villain to walk off with freely offered items in New York City. Remember that fact when you want to show off your 'cool' new situation to Little Sister Susie. This is *villainy school*, not a warm and fuzzy Charles Dickens novel."

wasn't big on farewells.

"Little bro, I've got something for you!" Alex said with a smirk, the closest he ever came to a smile. He held up a single glistening quarter.

George sucked in a breath. This was no ordinary quarter. He'd heard the story a hundred times. When Alex had completed the bank heist for his capstone project, the school came to take their part of the money. He was left with only a single roll of quarters for a job well done. "Next time," the school official had said, "anything you earn will be yours to keep, my boy!"

The minute the council left, Alex had thrown the roll of coins across the room, causing an explosion of quarters like flashing silver confetti. All that work for a lousy ten bucks. And as a student, he hadn't even been qualified to apply for Distinguished Villain, even though his heist had been flashier and more complicated than many that had secured the plaque for others.

Calming Alex down had taken George most of the morning. Yes, Alex, the school was so wrong! Yes, Alex, everyone knows you're awesome! George had gathered all the quarters for him. Eventually, Alex had regained his self-control, but he was never quite the same. Since then, he used those quarters like talismans.

"This is my own lucky quarter," Alex said. "I had this on me the day of the big press conference after the bank job." His fingers slid along the metal before he dropped it into George's palm. "May it bring you as much luck as it did me."

George's throat tightened. His brother really *did* care for him. Affection was frowned upon among villains, but families were always important. No one else would ever watch your back like family. Alex would never hand over his lucky quarter to just anyone. He must believe that George was special.

Resisting the urge to hug his big brother, George just nodded and climbed into the car. His chest puffed out as they pulled away. At that moment, he felt sure nothing could stop him from graduating at the top of his class. All the years of being pitied by his parents and mocked by his brother—all of that was over. He'd finally fit in.

After a last hug from his teary-but-proud mother, he boarded his plane. George leaned his head against the window and watched his home shrink below him until it dwindled to a speck impossible to see even if he had worn his Mastermind Deluxe Goggles. He fixed his gaze on the horizon, waiting for his future to be revealed.

George was lucky enough to get a direct flight, so he would arrive in New York City early. Auditions began at 8:00 a.m. sharp, first come, first serve.

His throat tightened from more than just the rough flight into New York. Alex wouldn't share anything about what the audition would involve. He'd said, "They made us all swear The Oath to keep the trials a secret." His eyes had glinted. "And you know what The Oath means."

George did. The Oath was the one rock to stand on in the villain world. It separated the professional villains from the riffraff of petty thieves and basic criminals. With villains being so good at lying, they needed a way to ensure when one was telling the truth. Thus: The Oath.

All promises made with The Oath were as binding as Double Trouble Glue[4]. Villains caught violating The Oath were outcasts from professional villainy society, with

---

4   Goofy McGaff (formerly known as "Clever McGaff") once used Double Trouble Glue to scale the Empire State Building. He put glue on each finger, planning to climb straight up the outside wall like a certain unmentionable superhero. He got about ten feet up before the glue dried. Five hours later, police removed a windowpane from the building with Goofy still stuck on there like a squashed fly. They carried him right into custody.

Academy status revoked. No one *ever* broke The Oath.

George knew their father had even gone to jail because of his sidekick's error yet hadn't hung his sidekick out to dry. Villains and their sidekicks swore never to rat on each other if one got caught. In their own way, villains were very honorable.

That peculiar honor allowed villain parents to trust the Academy with their precious offspring. The Academy would be sending a shuttle to the airport to pick up a handful of potential students arriving around the same time as George. He anxiously wondered what they'd be like. Would they be different from the villain kids back home? After Dad's jail sentence, Mom had kept the family pretty close to home until Alex went to school.

When the plane landed, George squeezed his new lucky quarter, thankful that Alex believed in him.

In the airport, George felt like a pebble swooped up and carried along a speeding current. Nothing in Omaha had prepared him for the sheer size and energy of New York City. He rolled his heavy suitcase to the shuttle bus area, panic nipping at his heels. How would he even know which bus to take?

A group of kids around his age stood at the far end

of the airport shuttle service lane. Two wore long black cloaks. Another had dark sunglasses. A girl with a sleek black bun leaned against the wall but somehow radiated danger. None of them were speaking to the others, but all were casing the joint. Their gazes roved constantly, no doubt collecting intel on security cameras and police officers with the casualness of a long-standing habit.

George fought a grin. He was pretty sure he had found the right shuttle stop. Just as he walked up, a sleek gray shuttle bus without any markings pulled up in front of them.

A bald man in a dour, dark suit stepped off the bus. "If you are here to audition at the Academy…" He paused, glaring, before continuing. "Step on the bus."

The bristly teen with the sunglasses was the first to step on board. The rest followed. George took an empty seat midway back, happy to have a window seat.

As the bus smoothly merged into traffic, the man stepped into the aisle. He was tall and wore wire-rimmed glasses. He looked like every businessman ever.

"Hello, prospective students," he said in a booming voice that made George wince.

The man spoke into a little microphone that amplified his voice. A lot. "You will be called *ghosts*. You will say nothing and touch nothing unless invited to. Get used to it."

He adjusted his glasses. "You could also be booted out by tomorrow, so if you ever wanted to visit Central Park, the Statue of Liberty, or anything else, this is your chance. Though why you'd bother, I have no idea. Beautiful architecture, fabulous history, yada yada, blah, blah, blah." He waved his hand in the air, squinting at each student like a pirate on an especially bad day.

"Some things you must remember," he continued. "Masses of tourists swarm through those locations taking photos, so be discreet. Be sure to utilize basic deflection skills that suggest to any concerned RPC that you are the child of a nearby adult. If you get your photo taken while pickpocketing or any other such trifling thievery while here, you'll answer to the Head Chancellor. We must keep a very low profile to protect our school against superhero invasion. In fact, we ensure this area of town is safe for tourists to keep the cops from coming around too often. Don't worry—if you stick around, you'll get plenty of opportunities for wrongdoing and villainy while here. We hope you'll have a fabulously wretched stay with us, one villain to another. But don't ask me for any help. My job here is done."

George swallowed hard, suddenly feeling like an RPC at a villainy convention. *This* was the welcoming committee? *Well*, he told himself, *this* is *a school for villains*. If he was looking for smiles and laughter, he was in the wrong place. But this was where he wanted to be. *Right?*

A tiny, little turncoat voice in his mind tried to whisper that perhaps a nice trip to a comic store might be a better destination, but George silenced that thought so ruthlessly that his mother would have been in awe. This was his family's heritage. He didn't need a friendly welcome. He raised his chin and looked back out the window.

The bus turned a corner, and light streamed into the shuttle bus. He gazed out the window and had to swallow a gasp as the view grabbed him by the throat. Silver skyscrapers reached to the sun. Greenery dotted the sidewalks. Flowers bloomed in window boxes.

George smiled at the sight of a woman in a business suit as she walked three busy poodles down the street. Actually, it looked like the dogs were walking *her*, tugging her along on her high heels. He almost giggled but caught himself, glancing around to see if anyone had noticed. He let out a small breath when he saw the other students were too busy staring out their own windows to notice him.

George took a minute to check out the competition. About ten other kids spread throughout the bus. None of them talked. The kid across the aisle had dark hair hanging in his eyes. He reminded George a little of Daniel, though this kid gazed only straight ahead. It seemed a very villainous thing to do.

George tried the stern pose for a minute. Then he looked back out the window, drinking in the excitement of being in New York.

Not being able to see the horizon was strange. He was used to the land stretching on and on until it met the sky. New York City felt very crowded in comparison, but he didn't mind.

There would be no chance of being bored here. No way. The Big Apple was a place full of people and things that George knew would be awesome. All he had to do was pass his audition, and this would be his new home for the next few years.

CHAPTER 5

THE ACADEMY

THE SCHOOL LOOKED surprisingly non-evil on the outside, just one more towering, gray building sandwiched between other towering, gray buildings. Superheroes couldn't know where all the villains were getting trained, though. Of course not. But once inside the plain silver office building with the tiny sign The Academy on the doors, a whole other world awaited.

The other prospective students—*ghosts*, George reminded himself—sailed through the doors like they owned the joint. Trailing behind them, George gripped the handle of his brand-spanking-new suitcase with sweaty palms. He reminded himself that it was normal to feel a little nervous, even with a lucky quarter to help out. He'd waited a long time for this day.

Pushing through the revolving doors and wheeling his suitcase behind him, he staggered into the cavernous main hallway of the school. Freezing air conditioning cooled his red face and blew his curls into a wild bird's nest. He patted down his hair and took a moment to soak in this long-sought-after sight.

Muted echoes of professional-sounding conversation floated in the tall, open atrium of the lobby. Ladies in tapping tall heels swished past, and old men with canes sat in table corners, hunched over tablets and laptops, phones pressed to their wrinkled ears. The whole room was sleek and silver, full of calculated precision like the shifting gears in an old-style watch. Nothing looked villainous at all.

He wasn't sure if he was relieved or disappointed.

Following the other kids from the bus, George walked to a table with a sign that read, *Prospective New Students Here*. Two boys sat behind the table, both looking too old to be current students. They were probably graduates, maybe sixteen years old or even older, with five o'clock shadows, even though it was only 11:00 a.m. One wore unrelieved, stark black. The other wore a pale-gray jacket zipped up to his neck. He looked ready to break something. Hopefully, he wasn't hiding a weapon under there.

George held tighter to his suitcase handle and took a deep breath. He tried to stride to the table with confidence, but the best he could do was keep from wobbling as he walked. The wheels of his case sounded ridiculously loud. The two boys watched him with dark eyes, not cracking smiles. No smirks. No mocking snickers. Just pure evil.

When George reached the table, his suitcase handle slipped out of his hands and the case dropped forward, landing on his foot with a thud. He bit his lip to stop himself from yelping, but he was sure he looked like a big doofus.

A duck could have been smoother, he thought with disgust. *That could be my villain name. Dastardly Duck Man! Look out! He'll drop his suitcase on you!*

"Name?" asked the boy in black. His lips had yet to smile, not even at the accidental suitcase slapstick routine. If this was an example of what George could expect to be like when he graduated, he felt pretty hopeful. The school *did* have a reputation for producing the most unforgiving, intense villains in the world.

"George Pruwell." He was thankful his voice didn't squeak.

"Pruwell? You're Alex Pruwell's brother?" the boy asked, eyebrows shooting up in clear disbelief. He looked George up and down and exchanged a glance with the other guy, who shrugged.

George sighed and nodded.

He'd known the comparisons to Alex would happen, but George had hoped they wouldn't start quite so soon. He supposed it was better than pitying comments about his dad, though.

The boys made a few marks on some forms, checked in his suitcase, and handed George a stack of papers. "Take these over to Stairway A and go down one floor. Go to the second room on your right," the boy in the jacket said, pointing down at a steep stone staircase just behind him.

George blinked at the unexpected sight. The stairs looked like they belonged in an old castle, built of stones stained and worn smooth from years of use. Behind him, sunlight gleamed in the clean office-like entryway. Glass panels soared above in the atrium's skylight. The old stone stairwell before him seemed as out of place as a snake in a room full of floppy-eared bunnies.

His feet seemed heavier as he approached the steps. Spiderwebs hung from the corners by the entrance. The air swirling out from the stairwell felt chilly and damp, and darkness cloaked the bottom steps. He tried to shrug off his anxiety. Alex hadn't shared much, but George knew enough to expect that the hardest challenges of his life awaited at the bottom of these stairs.

He eased into the dim stairway, trying to ignore the herd of kangaroos bouncing around in his stomach. As he descended, he tested each step with his toes before putting his full weight on it. His brother had often loosened stair steps for fun until George had started sliding down the banister to avoid the whole problem. As he crept downstairs, his nose twitched from the musty scents of long-forgotten basements and moldy parchment paper. He sighed with relief when he reached the bottom. The air conditioning must have turned off, because he found he was dripping with sweat.

Torches lined the hallway. The flickering lights somehow emitted neither smoke nor heat. Ornate runes covered the second door to his right. He didn't know any of these mystical shapes, despite his careful study of *Cracking the Code: Symbols for Sorcerer Wannabes*[5].

---

5   Excerpt from *Cracking the Code*: Jealous of how impressive sorcerers appear? Gnash your teeth no longer! You, too, can glower as you scrawl practically illegible symbols of power! Any combination of the symbols in this book will create results, assuming you have even a drop of mystical power. Use symbols with caution. Combine them at your own risk. (*Note: We are not responsible for anyone accidentally being turned into newts, frogs, or spiders.) Complete magical nulls might as well save their money, though. You can't force poo from a rocking horse.

His family lineage had always included mechanical villains or evil brainiacs rather than sorcerers, anyway. Dad had been a genius-level safecracker, lacking any drop of mystical power. Alex was an expert computer hacker, though he was determined to master multiple paths of villainy. George would be happy with just about any villain career type as long as he had a real villain job.

He stepped through the doorway into a perfectly square room empty of all furniture except one dark wood table with a single unlit candle on it. The floor and walls were stone like the hallway, continuing the impression that he had somehow walked into a castle. He couldn't believe he was actually beneath a skyscraper.

Stunned, George looked around, wondering what to do next. His grip on the papers loosened, and they slipped a bit in his hand. *Whew, caught them.*

Unfortunately, right at that moment, a dark figure appeared, literally out of nowhere. George jumped and dropped everything. The two stared at each other. The only noise in the room was the sound of papers sliding along the stone floor.

The man's face was hidden in the dark cowls of his priestly-looking robe. Long tassels with little bells hung from his woven belt. George's mother's shop did not sell robes like these because their owners were required to create them from their own magical powers. The more detailed the robe, the more skilled (and more dangerous) the sorcerer. This robe was very, very detailed.

The air conditioning kicked on again, a soft hum, and the tiny bells from the mystery man's belt chimed in the slight breeze. The air dried some of the sweat on George's forehead. He'd never felt so thankful for air conditioning.

"You must be George." The man sighed. "Go ahead and pick those up."

George had not expected an English accent but was proud he took it quite in stride. No reaction. Straight face, just like the boys at the registration table. He was getting better already.

"Yes, I'm George Pruwell."

The man waited, tapping one foot poking out from the long black robe, while George hurriedly picked up his paperwork, edges sticking out every which way. His hands left sweaty blots on the papers. His moment of pride was gone, as if written with Dynamo Disappearing Ink.

This wasn't going at all the way he had imagined. Why hadn't his brother at least warned him there'd be *paperwork* on Day One? Surely, that wouldn't have broken The Oath? George wasn't any good at organizing things, especially paperwork. He'd barely passed his co-op computer science class last year because he'd kept losing all the assignments. And, okay, he wasn't so hot with encryption or hacking, either.

"You're eleven, correct?"

"Yes, sir. Eleven and a quarter," George replied, standing as tall as he could. He was one of the shortest kids he knew.

The man shook his head, jingling the little bells on his robe more. When he pushed back his hood, his narrowed ebony eyes made George feel like a mouse that had just been sighted by a hawk. Coils of jet-black hair draped past the man's shoulders, with bits of metal braided into the strands. Power radiated from him. Even without the robe, any villain would know he was a Sorcerer.

"Before you begin at the Academy—*assuming* you do—we must ensure you are indeed fit for Trial Week. It's very challenging, as you know. I assume you have read your entire letter of welcome?"

George nodded. He had. At least once. He'd kept getting stuck on that one glorious sentence: *You are invited to audition for an exclusive spot in our villain trainee program...*

"Good. Then you know you must first pass at least one of a series of basic tests before you may even compete for a spot at the Academy during Trial Week. If you do not show sufficient talents for evil, you will be sent home tonight."

Wait, what? He had to pass a test to even take the next tests? He must have skimmed over that part in his excitement. A chill raced through George. Go home? Sent back in disgrace *tonight*? He wouldn't allow that to happen. He would be as evil as he could be!

Just look at his family tree, for Judas's sake! His aunt was an internationally known forger with thousands of perfect signature duplications, which included several heads of state. His grandfather had once been known as "The Fastest Villain in America." And, of course, there was Alex the Terrible, George's own brother. George would fit in at the Academy better than a bat in a belfry. "I understand, sir."

A clipboard and a black pen suddenly appeared in the man's hands. He *click-clicked* the end of the pen so it was ready to write and then looked expectantly at George. "Very well, then. Go ahead and light this candle."

CHAPTER 6

THE AUDITION

GEORGE LOOKED AROUND the room. The sorcerer wanted George to light the candle? With what? There was nothing here besides the candle on the table.

"Uh, sir…?"

"Chancellor Faust, George. I'm one of the headmasters here."

"Uh, okay." George's brain was too busy working out the dilemma of lighting a candle without a lighter or match to reply with anything wittier. Was he supposed to attack the teacher and find a heat source on him? But attacking a teacher seemed unwise, especially on the first day.

George racked his brain. Maybe this was some sort of trick test! Like, if he didn't attack, they'd know he wasn't evil enough!

Panic swelled around his throat until he heard a slight wheeze. He hated that wheeze. "You sound weak,"

Alex always said.

"With your *mind*, George," Chancellor Faust ordered. "Light the candle with the power of your mind alone." He sounded bored. At least he wasn't laughing.

By now, the giant rivers of sweat pouring from George's brow threatened to turn him into a human waterfall. He knew he had to look ridiculous, but Chancellor Faust hadn't cracked a smile. Did top villains even laugh? George couldn't remember the last time Alex had let loose a guffaw. No chuckles, either. Only the occasional sneering jeer.

George just stared. "I... I can't."

The chancellor said nothing but stared at George for the longest minute of his life.

He wasn't sure what to expect now. Would they kick him out now? But that wouldn't make sense. He knew well and good that his brother didn't have the ability to shoot flames out of his eyeballs or anything like that.

Chancellor Faust made a few notes on his clipboard, took the paper, tore a pink duplicate copy from the back of it, which he handed to George, and said, "I'm not surprised. Not many are accepted as sorcery villains, unfortunately. It's getting rarer and rarer and is usually passed down genetically[6]. Such ability would not guarantee a final placement at the school even if you had it. However, if any of the abilities tested today suggest you have profitable skills to build on, your odds of becoming a member of our school increase. Your next test is three doors down to your right."

Then the sorcerer vanished without a sound, as if he'd never even been there.

George blinked rapidly in relief. He patted the pocket that held Alex's—now George's—lucky coin, comforted by its slight weight. *I didn't want to be a sorcery villain anyway*, he assured himself. They usually ended up living in drafty old castles, stealing secret documents via dull sorcery spells or kidnapping foreign dignitaries for ransom in

---

6   Sorcery Villains: *The Simple Guide to Careers in Villainy* says, "Sorcery villains have long been associated with magic and dark arts, though our scientists have concluded such power stems from simple extrasensory perception ability, genetically based. However, to increase their intimidation factor, most sorcerers prefer to be referred to as 'magically talented,' not 'psychically talented.' A small distinction, except perhaps to one Arthur Grid, who called a sorcery villain "just a chick with an extra big brain." Mr. Grid was transported by the sorcery villain into the world's largest vat of brains, in the possession of a mad scientist villain, who then used Mr. Grid for parts. All of that to say: Call them 'sorcery villain,' and keep quiet unless you are a stronger villain than they. And possibly even then.

lieu of the princesses their forebearers used to take.

Then George sighed. *I'm not even good at lying to myself*, he thought sourly. Who was he kidding? A magical power like shooting flames from his fingers would be amazingly cool. He'd have loved to be a sorcery villain, but at this point, he'd be perfectly grateful to have a basic fraud specialist desk job in the city. He was growing more worried that getting the invitation to try out might be the closest he ever got to being a student at the Academy.

As he left the room, George passed another student. George recognized him as the kid across the aisle on the shuttle. Something about him still brought Daniel to mind, even though this boy had a cool, intimidating vibe that George's friend back home could never pull off.

The boy's smooth black hair fell around his dark eyes like a cloak. His trench coat brushed the top of combat boots. A good look for a villain, but the boy was chewing on his bottom lip so hard that it looked like it might bleed any minute. Hopefully not. George didn't do well with blood.

Pity stirred in him for this scared kid, who was also probably eleven years old, even if he stood a solid foot taller.

"Good luck," George whispered to the boy, realizing his mistake when the other boy's eyes popped open wide.

The Academy was probably recording everything they said or did. *Dang it!* He shook his head and kept walking, not looking back.

George blinked in surprise when he stepped into his next assigned room. Fluorescent lights glared from a ceiling covered in modern white acoustic tiles. The room was an electronic garden for any techno-savvy villain, full of tables crowded with all kinds of computers, from tiny laptops to giant, old-fashioned desktops.

A huge digital timer on the back wall was set to five minutes. A woman sat in the center of the room in a single rolling office chair but without a desk. Her white hair was swept back into a bun, and she wore a dark-green business suit. A phone buzzed in her hand.

"Greetings, George," she said without smiling. "Your assignment is to crack the school's mock database and retrieve the names of the top three students based on their grades. You may choose any computer in the room from which to work. They have a variety of operating systems, since many computer hacker villains prefer one over another."

She unfolded from the chair, her unexpected height making George feel smaller than ever. A smirk flitted across her face. "Now I've got to answer this call."

She stepped out of the room through a door the same color as the wall. He hadn't even seen the door was there. Villains should always notice every escape route!

The timer on the wall began a countdown. Panic jolted George as he realized he only had five short minutes to hack into a database. Alex could have done it in two, probably, but George had never felt comfortable running through the minefields of computer technology. Still, he had to try.

He chose a laptop that looked like his at home, which was Alex's old, cast-off computer. Of course, a computer built by Alex four years ago was better than most current computers. George was no computer hacker, though. He was more of a wonder-what-that-button-does slacker.

The cursor on the screen waited, blinking at him patiently. Where to begin?

George sat at the rolling chair in front of the laptop, squishing slightly into its cushy seat. His gaze flickered back to the clock, already down to four minutes and thirty seconds. He cracked his knuckles because that was what Alex always did before he got to work. George took a deep breath.

He clicked on the internet button and ran a search for the Academy of Villainy and Wrongdoing. The correct link came up immediately, much to his relief. The homepage only showed the name as the Academy, as if it was a regular private school. That was just a cover to keep its real mission undercover. Anyone in the world of villainy knew how to access the real information.

George clicked on the *log-in* button at the top. It asked for his username and password. He licked his lips. This was it. If he logged on as the school's Head Chancellor, Chancellor Levett, using SQL injection, he should be able to access any data he wanted. Surely, there were other people who would also have total access, but George didn't know their names.

He typed a select-user statement but couldn't quite remember if that's what Alex used. George had never tried to break into anyone's database, and it looked like today would not be the day he did so. The screen flashed a red box that read, *Invalid Username*.

George checked the timer. Two minutes, thirty seconds.

He clicked to log on again. He knew there was some special trick to using that button. A hundred other tricks probably existed to get to the database, but this was the only hope he had. Sweat trickled down his ribs. He thought furiously, feeling like his brain was a hamster on a wheel, racing but getting nowhere.

His fingers slipped on the keys as he tried the select query again. He managed to type another select-user phrase, hoping it might hack into the system. But once more, the computer flashed *Invalid Username*. This time, a smaller box popped up in the bottom corner.

George leaned forward and read it out loud. "'Your time is almost out. Luckily, this room will not self-destruct if you fail, so things could be worse.'"

George couldn't take a scrap of comfort from the message, if indeed that was its purpose. More time had slipped away. Thirty seconds left. He could try one more time.

His fingers tapped quickly on the keyboard. Just as he hit *Enter*, the screen went dark. George stared in shock for a long moment, afraid he had somehow managed to hit the *off* button. He'd done that once in computer class during a final exam.

Then he realized silence filled the room. The low, steady hum of all the computers was so familiar, he hadn't even noticed it until it had stopped. All the computers were off. The clock showed 00:00. He had failed. Again.

George drew in a shuddering breath. He staggered

upright when the woman walked into the room again. She already had marked something in red ink on his form. Her lips were a thin line.

She said, "Obviously, you have failed this test. We have a three-strikes-and-you're-out policy with complete test failures like yours so far. You didn't even get close. You have one final chance to show you belong at Trial Week. Walk down the hallway, turn left, then right." The woman paused before walking back through the door. "Your next test must be successful."

She shook her head and left.

Panic raced through George. He had failed two tests! He might get booted out of the school before he ever got to audition! He dragged a shaky hand across his brow, wiping away the sweat. His paperwork was so smeared by now, it looked like bad modern art.

George took two slow breaths. He lifted his chin and wiped his hands on his pants. He would win this next time. Success would be his. He would become a student at the Academy of Villainy and Wrongdoing. He would not let himself fail again.

The final room had two long tables full of technological wonders that could've been straight from the most recent edition of *Tools of the Trade*, George's favorite popular catalog for villainy paraphernalia. George's fingers itched to touch them.

Closest to him was the Right-Write 2, a forgery pen that would memorize any signature it traced. A villain could turn it on whenever necessary, and it would write out a perfect replication. His brother had been dying for one, not having their aunt's talent for forgery.

Beside the pen sat a seemingly harmless pair of pink eyeglasses, the cat-eye type that little old ladies liked to wear around their necks. But these glasses would highlight any living thing in an infrared glow when worn. They were like 3-D glasses, only better. Very cool, though not George's style. What George really couldn't keep his eyes off was the ray gun at the end of the table.

The weapon wasn't just any ray gun. This was a ProDecimator. Top of the line, too, judging from its size and swanky, smooth looks. He looked around. He was still alone. This might be his only chance ever to touch such a fine ray gun.

Shifting his shelf of papers to his left hand, he

reached out with his other hand before he could stop himself. He smiled as he picked up the ray gun by its grip. It felt so good, nicely cool against his sweaty palm. Hefty, but not too heavy. He imagined aiming it at a superhero, lifting it to eye level and—

His papers began to slip again, and he clenched his fingers to hold on to them. His other hand—the one on the gun—tightened in response too.

A giant flash of light burst through the room. Smoke stung his nostrils. When his vision cleared, an undeniable dark burn mark showed on the wall.

George gulped, staring at the damage. His eyes were so wide that the air conditioning was drying them out. Before he could even think of a plan, the door opened behind him.

"Careful with that one," someone said with a dry voice. "It might burn all your nose hairs off, and that would smell terrible. Trust me, I know."

George whirled, holding the ray gun behind his back. The speaker was a man with a rounded face and body that brought to mind a teddy bear. He even had bushy brown hair and big fluffy eyebrows. He approached, laughing in an honest way that didn't sound at all evil. Music to George's ears. He gingerly pulled the gun out and offered it to the man.

"All the kids grab that one first. I really should disarm it. Actually..." The man tapped his chin for a moment. He reached over and pushed a red button on the side of the gun. "I think *you* should disarm it. As in, right now. In two minutes, it will explode."

Then the man gave George a charming smile— *what a fabulous tool that smile is for such a sneaky villain—* and walked out the door.

CHAPTER 7

THE UNEXPECTED TURN OF EVENTS

GEORGE HEARD THE click of the lock as the door shut. A red light flashed on the ray gun, and a high-pitched beeping sound blared with each flash. His hands fumbled, his nerves ratcheting up about ten notches past freak-out.

He took a deep breath and tried to calm down. He'd built things before, after all. His mother had given him manual after manual of *Build Your Own World Destruction Tools*. This task was definitely within reach.

Panic blossomed, but he pushed it away and tried to ignore the noise of the gun, the flashing lights. He cast his mind back to the last ray machine he'd tried to build. It had actually exploded. Probably because he'd put too much energy through the tubing at once. Maybe if he simply disconnected the light tube from the handle…

He poked his tongue out in concentration, pushing and pulling on the gun. Nothing happened. He could have created a salty oasis in a desert with his rivers of sweat today.

Finally, in desperation, he closed his eyes and released a long breath. He let his mind rest, not striving, not working. Then he remembered. His eyes flew open.

He spun the screws on the handle, allowing him to flip open the end. Carefully reaching inside the narrow chamber, he pulled out the Light Containment Device, or LCD. The LCD was the one part of a ray gun absolutely required for it to work. Without it, the light diffused and couldn't burn anything.

The beeps and lights turned off as if they had never existed, and a deep silence filled the room. George breathed a sigh of giddy relief.

"Very nice," the teddy-bear-like man said, adjusting the tie as he walked back through the door. "How did you know what to do?"

George blinked, nerves warring with pride. "Well, a ray gun is really just like a fancy magnifying glass, right?"

The man shrugged. "Is it?"

George paused, wondering if he was making a mistake, but, no, he knew he was right on this one. He might be Duck Man, but at least he'd have a smokin' hot ray gun to shoot while he fell over his own feet.

"Yeah," George replied, his voice stronger. "It is. I took away the part of the gun that bends the light into a single beam, like taking out the glass disc of a magnifying glass. Simple." He stood, legs wide, ready to argue but was surprised when the man clapped slowly.

"Well, well, well. Looks like you *might* have it in you to be a villain after all. Of course, you are a Pruwell, but you never know. Family heritage doesn't always run true."

Relief coursed through George. "Am I in, then?"

The man's eyebrows shot up. "*In?* Well, young man, your demonstration today in Mechanical Machinations has earned you the right to try our one-week prep course and *audition* for placement within our school, otherwise known as Trial Week. If you hadn't shown aptitude in any villainous skill, we'd have sent you home today. It was a close call."

George's blood froze a moment but thawed as the man continued.

"You're a null in the magical department and useless at hacking, but that's okay. Since you succeeded here, you're done for the day. Once we officially begin Trial Week tomorrow, we'll see how you do with a wide variety of villain skills. You've got one week to get enough points to qualify for one of our three levels of villainy training. Most students will make it into one of them, though there's always a few who don't. There are A, B, and C Rosters. Of course, you probably know all this from your brother. Most graduates share stories with families, even though we aren't supposed to. Perfectly villainous, of course."

George nodded, hiding the fact that he didn't know anything from his brother. But his mother had told him tons. The top kids were A Roster, the ones destined to be Best Villains of their Era. Alex had graduated as an A Roster villain.

B Roster was for middle henchmen and so forth. Your best bandits, or even seconds-in-command. These folks knew how to brick up someone's feet faster than they could make a hoagie sandwich, but they'd never earn a Distinguished Villain plaque.

Being C Roster was almost more of an embarrassment than anything else. These were the villains foiled by superheroes with depressing regularity. The best of C Roster ended up as villain sidekicks, a safe bet to never steal glory away from their boss. But *most* C Roster grads were goofballs, jokes in the villain community, serving the important purpose as decoys for the real professional villains. They were hardly better than the RPC criminals, lacking even distinguishing costumes, but some students were just happy to be in any of the three rosters.

George, though, swore right then that he'd be an A Roster student, like his brother, like his father, and like his aunt. It all started with making the right first impression.

He'd been planning this moment for years. Every villain needed a signature outfit, and he had a perfect one ready to go. He designed it himself. His mother hadn't been thrilled with it, but she'd agreed to let him embrace his own style. He was going to kick some serious tail tomorrow when the real auditions officially began.

George was shocked to see light still filled the sky, even in the shadows of all the skyscrapers. In fact, only an hour had passed from the start to end of his initial tryout.

He stood in the long line to get his temporary dorm assignment, knees weak with relief. He had passed his first big hurdle. So much excitement raced through him that he felt like he was wearing Fast Foot Slippers[7], but he had to keep it together, now more than ever.

The boy with the smooth dark hair from earlier stood right behind him. George managed not to say anything but raised his eyebrows in a silent question. The boy gave a casual nod that someone else might have taken to be an absentminded habit. But George knew the boy had just communicated that he had done well. George worked hard to not smile, happy to have found a friendly face here.

When George reached the front of the line, he was given his suitcase and a keycard that read 512, along with

---

7   From *A True History of Villains* by Only-the-Truth-No-Really-I'm-Not-Lying Smith, "Fast Foot Slippers are first seen in the Grimms' tale of *Snow White*. The stepmother wore red-hot iron slippers that forced her to dance until she fell down dead. (It's in there—look it up.) But the shoes weren't really hot, merely warm, and they actually made her feel *excited* while she danced her way into death. They were sorcerer-made, as you might imagine, but what the general public does not know is that Snow White was the sorcerer-villain who made them. She conned the prince into marrying her, too, and then ran off with her partner, the Huntsman, after liberating the prince's piles of gold from the royal coffers. Snow White was a smooth villain. Take my word for it: Anyone who can talk to animals is a sorcerer, and anyone *that* sweet and kind in the face of constant mistreatment has a hidden agenda. Snow was one of the first femme fatales, which became its own villainy path thanks to her wiles, along with the accomplishments of Cinderella, Rapunzel, and Sleeping Beauty, villains all."

a packet entitled *Welcome to New York, Prospective Student of Villainy*! Inside there were maps with short descriptions of the local area. George followed the pointed finger of the registration clerk and rode up the elevator to the tenth floor. The silence of the elevator soothed George's frazzled nerves, allowing even more excitement to bloom. He'd done it! He had completed the first step of his journey.

As soon as he let himself into his tiny single dorm room—one narrow bed, one desk, one window, blank white walls—he grabbed his phone. "Mom!" he shouted. "I had to take three tests just to get into the tryouts, but I did it! Now I just have to go through the auditions to see which placement I'll get!" Surely he'd earn enough for placement? He hoped so, anyway. The thought of not getting any placement was not even to be considered.

"Ooh, honey! I'm so glad you were so wonderfully terrible today! I knew you would be!" George heard Alex in the background mumbling, and then their mom added, "Alex says not to lose his coin."

As if he would do that! George patted the coin in his pocket, happy to have his brother's vote of confidence at long last. He didn't ask to speak to Alex on the phone, though. Alex was not a share-the-joy kind of guy.

George wandered over to his window. The people below looked action-figure-sized. Cars crawled along Fifth Avenue, bumper to bumper, but the green of Central Park splashed brilliantly amid the gray of steel and concrete.

Excitement surged through him. New York City was overflowing with famous sights and places. One cool thing about the Academy was that they allowed students to come and go as they pleased. Most of them were champions at sneaking around without being caught, anyway.

Flipping through the welcome packet, he scanned the places he wanted to visit. One location in particular rated top priority. A little voice in the back of his mind whispered that this was a bad idea. He should study. Practice. Plot devious plans.

Pausing, he shook his head. No. He'd done all that. He was ready. And now, he was going sightseeing. He grabbed his keycard and strode out his door.

In the hallway, he nearly bumped into the dark-haired boy again. He was coming out of the door next to George's.

"Oh, sorry," George apologized. "I'm just going out...uh..." He shifted his weight from one foot to another, uncertain how to finish his sentence. The welcome packet map was, no doubt, a tool to help students skulk around without getting lost, not so they could actually go *enjoy the sights*. Especially not the wholesome ones he'd selected.

The boy hesitated, then said, "I'm Sam."

"George."

Sam scanned the hallway before whispering, "So. I hear that the Statue of Liberty is really something else."

George managed to swallow his laugh. He'd planned on the Central Park Zoo first—*cute baby bears*!!—but Lady Liberty was a top choice too. He held out the flyer with the map. He had already circled Lady Liberty as a definite destination. It was such classic New York. So many movies included the monument. "Wanna go together?"

"I won't tell if you won't," said Sam. "Don't want to get a bad rep on the first day."

They shook hands on it, and the two of them hopped on the elevator.

Strangely, George did not feel like discussing their morning. He felt completely villained-out. All he wanted to do was sightsee a little, take in the views of New York City, see everything he'd read about in so many comics and books set in the Big Apple.

The boys walked down Fifth Avenue, passing

Grand Army Plaza. They didn't say much.

"Been to New York before?" George finally asked as a horse-drawn carriage coasted by. He wished he could pet the dappled horse. It was beautiful, but he couldn't dare, not now.

"Nope," said Sam, and that was all. Maybe Sam was having second thoughts about joining him. Or what if Sam was spying on him? What if he planned to tell the admissions people that George actually enjoyed sightseeing like RPC tourists? Unease curled in his stomach, but just at that moment, their subway entrance came into view.

All thoughts faded from his mind. This week was the first time he'd flown on an airplane or ridden on a bus. And now he would get to ride on a big-city subway.

The air in the tunnel was cooler and, honestly, kind of rank, but George didn't care. He wanted to study the little machine that spat out his ticket, but Sam hustled him through the turnstile. The boys hovered just close enough to a mom-looking lady to throw off a security guard before slipping into the first open subway car headed toward Battery Park, where the ferry to Liberty Island was located.

Examining the brochure, Sam said, "If we had more time, we could have hacked our way into the reservation system to get into the crown. You have to reserve those tickets way in advance."

George tugged on his collar. Maybe *Sam* could have hacked into the National Park System, but clearly, George had better plan on buying his ticket in advance if he ever wanted to get to the top of the Statue of Liberty.

Sam didn't seem to notice George's discomfort. He flipped the brochure over and said, "That's okay, though. I'm cool with just looking from the shore of Battery Park today. The ferry ride will take too long, I think. After we've officially started at the Academy, we can always sneak back, right?"

George nodded. "Sounds good to me."

Of course, Sam could have said they were going to swim to the island, and George would have said it sounded good. The words *After we've officially started at the Academy* had sent so much excitement rushing through him that he could barely sit still. He couldn't believe he was finally here, in New York City!

A man in a suit stood by one of the handrails, holding a little girl in a pink dress. She giggled, a sound like tiny bells. George had to smother his grin at her cuteness. Two teen girls were laughing in the next seats over as their friend snapped a picture. Their *I Love New York* shirts marked them as tourists for sure. George felt a bit smug that he blended in better than them.

At the next stop, a group of older boys walked in, the blast from the subway door blowing everyone's hair all over. Sam's smooth, black hair slid right back into place, but George knew from experience his own would be sticking up like a mad scientist's, which was not the villainy path he was after. He hastily contained his riot of curls, running his fingers through them and patting them down.

The group of boys looked to be maybe Alex's age, dressed in black. Could they be villains too? They talked in low voices and glanced back at George and Sam. Unease dripped down George's spine. "Uh, Sam? Should we get off at the next stop?" he whispered.

The last thing they needed on this trip was trouble. But it looked like it had found them.

CHAPTER 8

THE STATUE

SAM SAID, "STAY cool," and leaned back in his seat to stare at the boys with eyes that suddenly seemed very, very dangerous. A small can appeared in his hand with a spray nozzle—where had that been?

Sam handed George a piece of gum. "Quick—chew this," he said, as he popped a piece in his own mouth. George did the same, chewing fast, mint flooding his mouth.

With a quick nod, Sam gave two tiny squirts, and a faint scent of burned pizza filled the car. The teenagers looked away and headed toward the next car. One of them threw a last glance back at them but kept walking, looking almost confused.

George sniffed. He knew that smell, and not just because his mother burned pizza on purpose.

"Oh my gosh! Where did you get a hold of Befuddled Repellent Spray? Villain 411's been out for ages!" The gum came with the can, protecting users from the effects.

"My family's got connections," Sam said, brushing imaginary dust off his hands. The little can was already tucked back into his jacket.

George let out a long breath. He could never look so menacing. Jumping Jehoshaphat, he hadn't even thought to bring any of his villainy tools with him today! It was a good thing Sam was with him.

George said. "I thought for sure they were going to be trouble!"

Sam shrugged. "They didn't look like the sharpest lockpicks in the box, if you know what I mean. I didn't even use a full dose."

George tried not to stare, but he was in awe. Sam was what every aspiring villain should strive for.

Their stop took a while to reach. George felt too overwhelmed to try to start another conversation, so he entertained himself by imagining stories about all the people getting off and on the metro. Sam did his trick of staring straight ahead. How did he get so statue-like? He must practice regularly. That took serious dedication.

Voices and laughter floated through the subway

car. As they neared the island, the subway car got fuller and fuller. When the boys reached their stop, they followed the crowd that spilled out into the light.

Lady Liberty soared in front of them across the water. She was taller than George had imagined, even from this distance.

Sam said, "Oh man! It looks just like it does in all the movies!"

It did. It really did. Greenish in tone, fierce in expression, the Statue of Liberty was utterly, completely perfect. George wanted to buy one of those green foam crowns that looked like Lady Liberty's, but his school would assuredly take a dim view of such a goofy hat.

Sam cast an uncertain look at him. "My dad told me to come here. He wasn't always a part of the villain world, you know? Married into it. He worked as a lawyer for businesses with questionable ethics, though, so he was pretty much a natural when he crossed over."

"My mom did the same thing! Though she worked in a department store. Still does, only for villain-wear."

Sam's shoulders relaxed, and his hesitation evaporated. "Then you get it. You know what it feels like to have a foot in both worlds. Not every villain does."

George beamed. Maybe he and Sam had a good shot at being real friends, even in villain school.

Sadly, the tickets for the ferry to the island itself were already sold out for the day, but nothing could bring George down. He said, "That's okay. We can still see it pretty good from here."

The boys walked along the path that gave them the best view of the island. He carefully sidestepped a mother pushing a chubby-cheeked baby in a stroller and smiled at the baby's grubby fists waving a stuffed bunny.

George stood on his toes and gawked. Such a perfect tourist day.

"Wow, there's a lot of people here," Sam said. He could see better, being taller, but even he had to maneuver around adults for a better view.

George said, "The brochure says it's one of the most visited spots in America."

"I believe it. This is as close as we're going to get today. Here. Try these." Sam handed George a pair of binoculars.

George gasped. Those weren't just any binoculars. These were ViewPros, Gold Edition. They made his Mastermind Magnifying Goggles look like a toy from one of Daniel's cereal boxes back home (which George had always wanted to try—villain brand cereals had no toys, only booby traps).

George gripped the ViewPros carefully in suddenly sweaty palms. "Thanks," he said.

He had no idea where these had been hidden—maybe with the repellent spray—but he wasn't going to waste time asking now. George lifted the binoculars and peered through.

Behind the lenses of the glasses, his eyes grew wide. It looked as if he were standing right there on the island.

The gray pedestal lifted Lady Liberty high above the green grass of the small island. The gold of her torch shone in the sun, and a flag flew in the background. It looked like a postcard!

So many people had come here over the years, ready for a new home. In fact, years ago, the Pruwells had been new arrivals too. His great-great-great grandfather had been the first Pruwell to come to America and start fresh here, fleeing from a con gone bad. He'd been so thankful to be here.

Sam was reading from the brochure again. "There's a plaque inside the pedestal with a special poem. Oh, I know this line—the 'Give me your tired, your poor, your huddled masses yearning to breathe free' line! That's really famous."

George's chest swelled with a trembling sensation.

Your huddled masses yearning to breathe free.

Millions from all over the world, scared and alone—they'd found new hope here.

Awestruck, he glanced at Sam, ready to invite him to share the moment. The other boy had tucked away the brochure and was now staring across the water without any expression on his face. He'd put on shades (where did the guy keep all these things?) and looked as stern as Lady Liberty herself. Sam definitely didn't look moved by the thought of all the new lives that had begun here.

Awareness splashed George in the face. He shouldn't be feeling this way, either.

He and Sam had shaken hands to keep this trip a secret for a reason. Giddy tourist glee was beneath the dignity of real villains, for sure. Civic pride was a big no-no too. But even worse was compassion, which encouraged sacrifice for the common good and other unsavory ideas like that. It was all well and good for RPCs, but not for villains.

And this was why villains didn't come to Liberty Island like an Average Joe tourist.

George handed back the binoculars and swallowed

his surge of unacceptable emotions. He was going to be a villain. If he was serious about making his family proud, he should be grossed out at these feelings—if he had to experience them at all.

He didn't look back as they walked away.

The boys took the Metro back. Sam said, "So. One big New York thing off the list. We've got some time to kill before dinner. Want to wander around and check out some other stuff?"

George perked up. "Sure. If you want, I mean. If you don't think it'll get us in trouble with the school."

At least he kept the eagerness out of his voice. Maybe there was hope for him yet.

Sam said, "Well, if you think about it, looking around now would help us get a feel for the area for any future jobs." He sounded serious—but his eyes were twinkling.

George stifled a grin. Sam obviously wanted to keep on sightseeing, and this was his smart excuse. So, he was having fun too—he was just better at hiding it. George could really learn a lot from him.

George smiled and nodded. "Sightseeing for the

good of villainy. Let's go with that."

The boys wandered all over Manhattan for an hour, looking into every store just to see what was there. George managed to shake off his embarrassment at his sentimental Lady Liberty moment. It had just been a fluke. He made a mental note to avoid that particular tourist stop for future trips, which should solve that problem.

They stared into the display cases of fancy department stores full of jewels and dresses with sparkles. George wished he could take pictures for his mother, but Sam probably would think it was weird to take pictures of women's clothing. But one fancy dinner dress had silver running through it almost like spiderwebs, and George knew his mother would have loved it. With a few tweaks, it'd make a perfect villain outfit for someone like the Dastardly Damsel of Deception[8].

---

8   From *Top Villains to Know*: "The Dastardly Damsel of Deception pretends to be a rich heiress who was recently robbed when she is, in fact, a master thief of priceless antiques. Once her victim invites her in, she knocks him out cold with a memory-deleting potion of her own creation and absconds with his treasures. Her signature trademark is the spiderweb, which always appears somewhere on her clothing. Just like a spider's prey, her chosen victims never know what hit them. Editor note: Always beware of beautiful women sporting webbed designs."

Other shops held an astonishing array of candy. Blue, purple, pink, rainbow... George had never seen so much sugar in one place. The sweet scents floating from the store made his mouth water.

Sam ogled the candy, too, but opted not to eat any. "I can't afford to let anything sweeten me up, especially with the upcoming week," he said, meeting George's eyes. The seriousness in his expression contrasted starkly to the lighthearted laughter all around them. "You know we still have a long way to go, right?"

George nodded hard enough to make himself dizzy. "Oh yeah, I know, sure."

But he hadn't really considered the upcoming week. He'd wanted a break, but if villainy was going to be his way of life, well, there would be no escaping, no days when he could act like any normal RPC enjoying the big city.

Suddenly, the brilliant colors of the candy seemed grayer. The fun bubbling inside George like fizzy soda pop seemed to leak out of him.

"Time to go," George said flatly.

Sam nodded. They didn't speak on the way back to the dorms, but Sam paused in front of his door.

"Thanks for going with me today," Sam said quietly,

after looking up and down the hall for eavesdroppers. "It would have been boring to just hang out around my room, which is what I probably would have done if I hadn't run into you."

George was uncertain what the appropriate response would be for a real villain. Should he be calm and cool? Disdainful? It made his head hurt to ponder all the possibilities. Whatever the right response was, George gave up trying to figure it out. He just told the truth. "I'm glad too."

It was quiet in his room. When they officially made it into the school, they'd get a roommate, but for now George was thankful for some time alone. He was exhausted from his travels, his tryout, and his time being a tourist. He wasn't sure Sam counted as a friend, exactly, but he wasn't just an acquaintance anymore, either.

Well, George would have to wait and see. He trusted others too fast. That's what Alex was always telling him. He'd say, "Look, Dad trusted that lousy sidekick of his, and see where that got him? Trust *no one*, George. *No one.*"

Alex was a real downer sometimes. George wondered if his brother had ever wandered through the streets of New York just for fun. If so, he'd never told

George about it.

George took a shower as hot as his skin could handle. After he was adequately clean and his skin as pink as a New York-style boiled hot dog, he collapsed in the bed.

He felt better knowing that another student here at least knew his name. They weren't real Academy students yet, but they were on their way.

The next morning, George woke up before the sun had crept past his curtains. Tucked warm in his blankets, he stared at the ceiling. This was it. Time to prove he was ready.

He pulled on his villain outfit. His reflection in the mirror made him smile. No, on second thought, he should glare, he reminded himself. Glare and glower. He had smiled too much yesterday as they'd toured the city. His face picked up bad habits quickly.

He practiced a little, lips pursed as he tried to look fiercer. He struck a fighting pose, or what he thought might be a fighting pose: arms raised and ready to attack, feet wide, knees bent. He looked awesome.

Black tights with red-and-orange flames crawling up his calves to his knees. *Check.*

A skintight black shirt with long sleeves all the way down to the wrist. *Check.*

Soft, black boots with thick soles. *Check.*

No cape yet, but one day he'd be able to afford a black one with red flames all over it. After a moment of panic when he realized his awesome outfit had no pockets[9], he tucked his lucky quarter in his boot just in case. He didn't believe in luck, not really. But still, it felt better to have the coin within reach.

When George walked over to Sam in the dining area of the dorm, Sam gawked, losing his usual poker face. He was already in the section reserved for villain trainees and prospective students.

"That's what you're wearing today?" Sam asked, shock clear in his voice.

---

9   The Super's TV Network show *Stitchery Witchery* addressed the problem of pockets in a clip by host Emmi Broider. "A lack of pockets is a very common costume design failure. Sure, you may be streamlined during flight, but where are you supposed to keep your good luck charm, your safecracker, or, if you happen to be a superhero, your inflated ego? In your SHOE? Ha ha! Some things might fit there, but, villains, do you want your tiny potion bottles to smell like your feet? What hapless sap would drink those expensive potions, then? Let us also not forget we must remain light-footed (and light-fingered) as we go about our jobs! Hard to do that with a Mini-Syringe Kit stabbing you in the toe. No, pockets are vital!"

George shifted his feet, glancing down at his legs. He thought the flames showed up nicely against the menacing black tights. "What's wrong with it?"

Sam rolled his eyes, but a smile twitched at the corners of his mouth. "Nothing—if you want to spend your best villain days kidnapping old ladies' cats for twenty bucks ransom." He waved his hands across his own outfit. "Now *this* just screams death and destruction."

George was impressed by Sam's black leather pants and matching jacket. The black boots looked great too. Even the silky black button-down shirt was slick.

"And check this out!" Sam turned his head to one side and then whipped his face to the front again, causing the long bangs to slide over his face like a curtain.

It worked. Definitely villainous.

"Very cool," said George. Suddenly, he wasn't so sure about his flame tights. He'd had them planned since he was five. Maybe that was part of the problem?

If only he didn't seem so awkward all the time! If he wasn't careful, he'd end up on the C Roster for sure. Maybe Sam could help out, though, and give some advice. He sure seemed to know his stuff. He'd also proven yesterday he wasn't too strict about the whole never-have-a-friend rule most villains followed.

"Let's do this!" George said. He raised his hand for a high five.

Sam sighed. "Look, George. Stop being so friendly and nice. Especially around here. It'll keep you out of A Roster faster than anything else."

George flushed, dropping his arm back to his side. His hand felt like a dead fish on the end of a stick.

The only villainous thing he'd done right since he'd gotten here had been deactivating the explosive laser gun. He held tightly to that soothing memory. He had talent. They wouldn't have let him stay if he didn't. But still... he looked at Sam, so slick and evil. That was a high standard to meet.

The boys shuffled through the cafeteria line in silence, filling their trays with full-of-fiber granola that actually seemed to have small sticks in it. Both boys chose steamed kale as a side dish. Sam poured a cup of dark, bitter coffee, but George stuck with water. No fruit, no pastries. Not here.

George had never had anything like a pastry. He'd been secretly hoping to sneak some at a New York bakery, but now that he really saw the competition, he realized he'd better not. He was going to have enough trouble without adding sweetness.

The boys took seats next to each other at the end of a long table full of sleepy-looking kids. No one seemed to be paying any attention to them.

"Uh, Sam?" George asked.

Sam flicked his hair out of his eyes. "Yeah?"

"How did you do in the pre-screening tests?" George hadn't wanted to ask yesterday, but he was burning with curiosity after seeing Sam in his villain costume.

Sam shrugged. "Not bad. I got the candle to flicker. The robe-dude seemed pretty impressed with that."

Suddenly, taking a gun apart seemed totally insignificant. Any nerd with a book could figure that out. A real villain, though… the kind with sorcery powers, who fought all the biggest, baddest superheroes… that would be amazing.

Not even George's brother was a sorcery villain. Alex could fly really well with his electromagnetic cape, break into any almost safe, and decode every computer problem he had ever come across. George had once been determined to beat his brother's success. Now, as he watched Sam chow down on rock-hard granola *with extra twigs*, George wondered if maybe he had set himself the wrong goal.

With a shake of his head, George reminded himself that he belonged here as much as anyone else. He was fine. This was all fine. He just had to be on his best worst behavior, and it would all work out. Hopefully.

CHAPTER 9

THE PROSPECTIVES

THE FIRST MORNING of Trial Week began with an assembly of all the prospectives. George shifted uncomfortably in his seat. The audience of fellow ghosts was a sea of almost completely unrelieved black. Black turtlenecks, black cloaks, black suits, black hats.

George felt ridiculous in his skintight top and flame tights, but it was the only costume he had. He slumped in his seat and crossed his legs, trying to hide as much of the brilliant colors as he could. Sam was four seats over but hadn't done anything other than offer a brief nod when they both sat down.

Over a hundred new applicants had passed the pre-screening. George had no idea they'd invited so many people. He sighed. Competing against so many kids for a prime spot in the school rosters looked tougher by the minute.

He sat up straighter when Head Chancellor Levett approached the microphone. The small amounts of rustling in the crowd faded. Chancellor Levett wore a black suit with a black tie over a black shirt. One bright-red carnation peeked out from his breast pocket, but otherwise, he was a shadow. When he stood completely still, George found a strong need to blink to make sure he was still seeing the man.

One of Levett's talents included practically disappearing while standing in plain sight. He had never been caught, not once, in all his years of stealing precious treasures from heads of state. Rumor said he could make things levitate. George didn't know about that, but he could see now why this man never got caught. Perhaps it was just excellent camouflage against the black curtains behind him on the stage. George wished more than ever he had thought to wear different attire.

"Greetings, future villains," Levett rolled out, his voice deep and rich.

A thrill chased along George's spine. One of the best villains of all time had just called him, George Pruwell, *a future villain*. His worries faded. Anything was possible, after all.

"As you know, everyone in this room has already displayed at least the *potential* for villainy. In fact, you would not have been invited to even audition."

He looked down his nose at the students in the front row before moving his gaze row-by-row across the audience as he spoke. "While you are a student, however, be sure to know that we are here to teach you villainy, not to coddle you. In the coming week, you will attend classes and physical exercises for the purpose of determining your potential. Some of you might be ready for more advanced coursework than others. It suits no one to study at the wrong level. In the unfortunate event that someone needs to be dismissed altogether, we will speak to you privately."

Suddenly, he clapped his hands twice, making George and most of the other students jump in their seats.

"Please rise to take The Oath for your student behavior."

George shivered. The Oath was serious business.

"I—state your name—"

George said, "I—state-your-name—" His words were lost in a sea of student names being spoken and he kicked himself for his rookie mistake. He listened harder.

"Do solemnly swear to study villainy and wrongdoing to the best of my ability."

George swallowed. This was the moment. "Do

solemnly swear to study villainy and wrongdoing to the best of my ability."

"I promise I will not reveal any of the secrets I will learn about the Academy this week, to include its location, coursework, staff, or student body."

George could promise that with a light heart.

"Even if I do not graduate from this school."

George repeated this last phrase with a frown on his face.

A moment of silence filled the entire auditorium when they were done. A small smile crossed the chancellor's stern face. Then he said, "Go on and give yourselves a hand."

The audience broke out in polite applause. George clapped loudly with relief.

Teachers passed out schedules down the rows of students. The woman from his hacking trial took the microphone. George burst into sweat just looking at her, flashing back to his failure in the computer room. "These are your classes. Please note that points will be awarded throughout the week, which will be used when determining your placement into A, B, or C Roster on Friday, or if you should receive no placement at all. Give it your best worst-villainy try!"

George had no more room for anything like his early failures this week. He had just one week to show them he was ready.

The first class of the day was Flight Gym, held in a giant underground cavern beneath the school. George's instructor was Chancellor Morgue. George had not seen her at any of the trials. She was small and delicate like a wren, no doubt making flying easier, but George didn't dare hope his small size would be helpful here.

When she introduced herself to the class, she said, "Be thankful you're my students. I'm the best flyer around and can show you tricks you haven't even dreamed of."

George felt his shoulders relax. Maybe this would be okay.

Chancellor Morgue continued, smoothing her gray hair. "Of course, my skills won't help you if you don't listen. I think they assigned me this teaching job in case any of you really crash—my name would just seem appropriate."

This comment did not help George's nerves. He had

seen Alex fly once using his electromagnetic cape[10]. George had certainly read a number of articles on it, clipped out by his mother from her favorite weekly newspaper, *All in the Family: A Lifestyle Choice for Villains*. But reading about capes and using them were two different things.

He was assigned to a small group of twenty students for the week. Sam was in the group, much to George's delight, but Sam studiously watched the chancellor and didn't look at George once. None of the other students met his eyes, either.

George turned his attention back to their instructor, who was explaining the basic construction of the cape. Flying capes came in a variety of materials such as silk, felt, wool, and leather, but the school's were a sturdy, wrinkle-free cotton-poly blend.

---

10   From *Help! I Love A Villain!: A Regular Public Citizen's Guide to Understanding Your Beloved*. "Many RPC.s believe that superheroes and villains fly from innate powers, which seems intimidating. Villains often encourage this belief to make their jobs easier. However, it can help to know that with the exception of aliens (and we do not recommend dating an alien superpowered being because you will end up kidnapped as ransom far too often), most of us use electromagnetic capes to fly. Even *you* as an RPC. could fly when wearing one. Be sure to get instruction first, though. No sense in breaking a leg to avoid breaking your heart!"

The cape looked like any plain, black cape to George. Red flames would really add some pizzazz.

Chancellor Morgue clipped the cape around her neck with practiced ease. She then stood perfectly still, arms at her sides.

"Now, watch, class, as I let the cape's sensors know it's time to lift. Note that the pose unfortunately mirrors that of Captain Perfectus, the greatest superhero of all time, but that's just the way the capes work. Now, pay attention."

She raised one fist upward and rose gently five feet off the ground. Her gray hair floated as if in a breeze, though the humid air sat heavy like soup. The cavernous ceiling had stalactites on it, so George sure hoped no one got out of control and flew into one of those. He wondered if that was just part of the test. That would be one heck of a way to unenroll from the Academy's Trial Week.

George was so busy staring at the pointy, jagged edges of the stalactites way up high that he missed the instructor's directions to come get a cape. The stampede to grab one of the best took him entirely by surprise.

Belatedly, he took off running after them, but he tripped and fell. By the time he got to the cape room, there was only one left. Its edges were tattered, and it had at least a hundred rips repaired with clumsy stitches. It seemed to want to fly only counterclockwise, so George spent most of the morning flying in circles underneath the rest of the applicants, who zoomed around playing touch tag, except for the one poor kid who couldn't get off the ground at all.

"Lousy cape," George muttered. He tried to land, only to be jerked by the neck straight up to the ceiling. The stalactites loomed, waiting to stab him, but George managed to direct himself downward with his fist at the last second. Of course, he body-slammed into the cavern floor, but he hoped Chancellor Morgue was too busy demonstrating how to do loops to notice. He staggered to his feet, trying to look like he was swaggering instead of swooning.

The afternoon brought a challenge of a different sort. Stumbling to the next class, still dizzy from all the spins and dips required by the flight examiner, they entered a long white room full of traditional school desks. The professor declined to introduce himself, handing out papers at the door. Instead of physically hard labor this time, the students were given page after page of math story problems which they had to solve using logic or intuition, whatever worked for them.

The two trains problem was a known torture device of small children in the regular public citizen schools, so George had long mastered that one. "If Train A is going toward Manhattan at fifty miles per hour while Train B is going away from Manhattan at seventy mph, at which train stop will they cross paths?"[11] Math had a lot in common with mechanical engineering, so his hope slowly rose once again. Maybe he could salvage this day.

Derek Smiley (poor guy, with a name like that) was having a rough time, though. His pencil lead ran out in the middle of the assignment. He was searching his bag with increasing panic until George couldn't stand it anymore. He dropped an extra pencil on the floor and rolled it over to the other boy's desk with a gentle kick. Derek glanced over his shoulder with the barest nod of thanks, shoulders stiff. The whole maneuver was impressively discreet and sneaky, but George still burst into sweat. He breathed easier only when minutes passed without the frowning instructor calling him out.

---

11   In real life, the answer to the train problem is this: It doesn't matter when they will cross, because it only matters which stop you need to get off at and how long it takes your train to get there. Who cares when the other train will fly by on the other track? No one.

Maybe the instructor had been distracted by the small red-headed girl next to him. She apparently couldn't even finish the assignment with or without her pencil.

He winced when she finally broke down in tears but didn't say a word. Her name tag identified her as Elizabeth Shade. George hoped she had flown really well to make up for her miserable performance now.

He figured his own chances had gone up, and he was feeling pretty good by the end of the day. Their points were to be posted daily in the dining room, so he'd find out soon. It couldn't be that bad on the first day.

Not even a dinner menu of Brussels sprouts soup sprinkled with stinky blue cheese could damper George's spirits. His mother loved to serve Brussels sprouts.

He filled his tray with a big bowl of soup in the cafeteria line before heading to the dining tables. When he entered the room, he stopped and gaped, soup sloshing.

Everyone's points were publicly posted on one wall of the dining room. The points were not just discreetly listed like he'd expected. Of course not. No, this was, after all, a training ground for all things villain.

Instead, points were displayed via a huge bar graph, showing each student's standing in comparison to everyone else's, including points earned (or not) for each skill. Every student's name was right there, visible to everyone, humiliating all the low-scorers.

But that wasn't the worst part. The name with the lowest points had a dunce hat glued over it for the day, courtesy of an Advanced Student who found the whole thing hilarious, as did his classmates.

George gasped a little with relief to see his name was *not* under the dunce cap. Everyone was checking for their name, some casually cool and others aggressively stalking up to the board, flipping over the food trays of several unlucky students.

Balancing his own tray with one hand (a dangerous move) George found his name near the lower middle of the list. Better than it could have been, all considering. His poor flying had definitely cost him, but no one must have seen him sending that pencil to Derek thankfully. And it was math for the win tonight! Sam had scored near the very top.

George felt bad for Anthony Snoodlecone, the boy who hadn't been able to fly during Cape Class. He must have failed the story problem too. The jaunty dunce hat sat boldly on top of Anthony's name card. Anthony gulped at the sight of it and hurried with a bright-red face to the far side of the cafeteria, by himself.

George took a step toward the poor guy when Sam passed by, heading the opposite direction with his tray.

Sam didn't even glance sideways but whispered, "Think twice."

The meaning was clear. George's career was on the line. With a sigh, he chose another table and ate alone. The soup reminded him of his mother. He missed her, but he couldn't admit that to anyone. It might cost him points.

CHAPTER 10

THE WEEK

AFTER DINNER, GEORGE stepped into the elevator with Sam. The doors closed and they were alone.

"You looked great during cape class," George said, because it was true. Sam was a natural up there.

"Well, at least you got off the ground," Sam offered. "That one kid didn't even do that. You've definitely got talent. Well-hidden, maybe, but it's there."

George grinned as Sam slugged him on the shoulder. He didn't dare laugh, even though he wanted to. "What about being too nice, Mr. Encouraging? You'd better watch out, or you'll lose points."

"I'm not worried."

If only George could say the same!

The first day of Trial Week left George more exhausted than he had ever been. He didn't even make the planned call to his mother but instead fell fast asleep, still in his flaming tights, before the sun had fully set.

The next morning, everyone ate breakfast in silence. Pickled octopus was offered as a delicacy, an expensive treat for villains. George decided it didn't matter how much it might improve his evil standing, he could not eat suction cups on tentacles. At least not before noon. He stuck with the ultra-healthy granola. He added a few extra twigs for good measure. Sam, however, ate two helpings of the slimy sea creature.

The morning session was Escapes, taught by an escape artist who went by the name the New Houdini. He had been taught all Houdini's tricks, or so he said, by Houdini's grandchildren. George did not remember hearing about Houdini having grandchildren. Since Delight in Deceit was on tomorrow's schedule, perhaps the teachers were setting them up for that class.

"If you're around when a security alarm goes off, you know that too many things have already gone wrong with your mission," began the New Houdini, with no other introduction. His long twirly moustache wiggled like a fish on a hook. "A good escape artist will see any errors that take place before the main system notices and will have an escape plan already in action. Today, we'll be inside a maze full of tripwires. Your job is to escape on foot before the timer runs out, without setting off any alarms. If someone else sets off an alarm, you must escape using your cape before the doors over the top of the maze close. The cape may only be used if an alarm sounds, not before."

George loved mazes. He often drew them at home. No doubt he would get tons of points this morning.

They proceeded to the middle of the maze, and George placed his left hand on the burnished silver wall. If he kept it there, always on the left-hand side as he walked, and turned only when his hand was forced around a corner, he would eventually find his way out. He was almost positive.

The instructor said, "Get ready. Get set. Go!"

Most of the students took off running willy-nilly, capes flapping, some to the right, some to the left, some to the path behind them. George didn't worry about them. With a nod to himself, he set off with a measured pace, the metal wall cool to the touch.

His face flushed with concentration. This time, George had managed to get a better cape, so he felt quite hopeful.

He reached the first T in the path. He kept his

fingers on the left wall, following his hand around the curve. He checked behind him. Sam was doing the same thing. George hid a smile. It felt good to have someone like Sam trust his methodology. George kept walking.

By this point, he could hear shouts behind him as students became completely lost in the maze. Some were talking together, but teamwork was frowned upon, so George kept to himself, though he wished he could tell them to follow him.

Suddenly, a blaring noise ripped through the maze. His heart thudded fast. Someone had tripped an alarm. The screeching of metal echoed as giant doors unfolded over the edges of the maze, beginning a slow reach toward the middle.

George stood straight, lifted one fist, and rose off the ground. His stomach swooped, and he wanted to shout with excitement. In seconds, he was above the maze, and almost in the clear—he just had to zip to the sideline now!

He glanced down to see Sam hot on his heels. Unfortunately, he also caught sight of Elizabeth, the girl who had cried during the math word problem exercise. Her cape was pinned in a metal claw that had popped out of the wall.

Elizabeth struggled fiercely, reaching toward the cape clasp at the neckline. But if she took off her cape, she'd never get out.

He was moving before he even considered what he was doing. *It's a good thing I got such a good cape today*, he thought to himself as he zoomed down into the maze to Elizabeth.

"Here!" he shouted over the alarm and the screeching of the closing doors. "I'll pry open the claw! You yank the cloak out."

His fingers trembled as they clasped the cold, steel pinchers, but he gritted his teeth, pulling with all of his strength. The jaws of the claw slowly opened, and Elizabeth pulled her cape free.

They both flew straight up, just missing the closing doors, and landed to the side of the maze. George grinned at her. She smiled back, tears still in her eyes. Then the booming voice of the instructor sliced between them.

"What do you think you're doing, Mr. Pruwell?" the New Houdini hollered. "*Rescuing* someone?" His voice got even louder. "If this had been a real situation, you both would have been busted by the police! *Never* go back for a fallen partner or sidekick. That's what The Oath is for—we know they won't betray us. But you can't bust them out later if you're tossed in a cell with them, now can you?"

George's face felt as though it was covered in the same red flames as his legs. He hung his head, struggling not to cry. Not here, not now. He'd made a major mistake.

The instructor sent him to the Prison Bench by the door for the remainder of the afternoon, so he couldn't earn any other points. Elizabeth failed the maze activity but was allowed to stay in the day's remaining trials.

George glared at the ground, sternly reminding himself over and over *not* to help anyone else again. He might have just blown everything.

"No more Mr. Nice Guy!" he whispered.

When George came into the dining room that evening and saw the dunce cap over his own name, he wasn't surprised. Sam kicked George in the leg when he walked by to sit down to eat. Code for *Sorry, but stop being so nice.*

He didn't need the reminder. Help no one. Trust no one, just like Alex said.

George glanced over at Sam. Did that include him? Hopefully not. George sighed. He'd be lonely if he couldn't talk to Sam anymore.

By the next day, thankfully, the dunce cap had moved to Serena Cards, who could not pass the lie detector test during their Deceit Lesson. George had lucked out. For his lie, he was told to say that he still played with plastic toy figures. Sometimes the truth worked better than a lie.

Day four of Trial Week found the dunce hat back to Anthony Snoodlecone, who had managed to lock himself in the safe instead of getting the jewels out. Very tragic. George had rocked out on the safecracking exercise, thanks to Dad's old textbooks he'd long ago memorized.

At the end of day five, though, the chart was gone.

George and Sam milled around with the other prospectives in the cafeteria, wondering what happened. Today was the last day of Trial Week. (Villains preferred five-day work weeks just like anyone else.) Points mattered more than ever.

Then a tall woman strode into the room, someone they had never seen before. Her black heels clacked on the floor, and blonde hair curved smoothly around her face. George was instantly reminded of his mother but pushed away the reminder of home. This was no moment to get sappy.

The woman held three pieces of paper. One was golden and actually shimmered. One was silver and glinted majestically. One was brown, not bronze, just a dull brown with no glow at all. Murmurs ran through the crowd as they realized what she held. The decisions were already complete. Those were the three rosters.

Fear suddenly gripped George so hard, he could barely breathe. Heat crept up his neck. Was his name on one of them? He felt pretty sure he had done well enough overall to get in B Roster at least, even with his errors. He hoped.

Please, please, be on A Roster! Even B Roster, but not C. Not C!

The woman reached the front of the room, and the students fell silent. They could have heard a lockpick drop. "After finding your name, please report to the instructor listed in bold print at the bottom of that roster." No one came near her while she taped up each list. Her aura of evil was quite scary, tidy hair notwithstanding.

Even once she stepped back, the kids moved like a herd of turtles in a mud puddle, until she said, "Oh, for the love of all that's evil, get on with it!"

The paralysis of the crowd broke. Everyone was running, jostling for position, even the coolest of the cool. Elbows connected with ribs, and muffled *oomph*s followed.

Sam and George exchanged a glance. They raced to the first list, the golden A Roster.

Kids read names aloud, the sounds overlapping to make a dull roar. George couldn't see anything from within the sea of students surging to find their names.

Finally, George and Sam reached the front of the crowd. George reached up one finger still sticky with broccoli jam from breakfast. Running his finger down the list, he left a brown-green smudge along one side.

"Nice going, loser!" someone said.

George jerked his hand back. He didn't give up his spot, though. He traced the list with his eyes.

Bryant... Collins... Crumwell... Forger (what a promising villain name!). Down the list he went, skimming through the LMNO part and then stopped at the Ps.

Pratt... Pry... Rembrant...

George blinked and looked again. Pratt... Pry... Rembrant. He felt like he'd swallowed a gallon of ice. Beside him, he heard Sam holler. "I made it!"

Sam smiled triumphantly at George, but when he saw George's expression, he quickly turned back to the list, skimming the rest of the way down. Looking back at George, Sam didn't say a word, but his eyes were sympathetic.

George stumbled away and pushed through the silver list throng. Surely, he'd be listed here. He'd gotten one of the top scores in safecracking! *Middle men*[12] *can always rise to the top if they work hard enough*, he reminded himself.

Quint the Ghost, an infamous villain who'd graduated from the Academy in 1999, had begun in B Roster but had been moved to A Roster after discovering he could walk his body through walls through some kind of molecular restructuring process. Hard to beat that superpower in a villain.

George steeled himself. *Come on, B Roster!*

Persimmons. Price. Rose. Runnings.

The world tilted beneath his feet, and his breath sped too fast. He looked from side to side and took in the small clump of unhappy students standing in front of the brown roster, which included Serena Card and Elizabeth Shade. His feet felt encased in concrete, but he managed

---

12   *Get a Job: A Guidebook for New Villains*: The Middle Man: Usually from B Roster, these villains are trusted with activities like bodyguarding, collecting the boss's money, and, if necessary, permanently removing nonpayment problems. We suggest Middle Men keep meticulous notes on all activities, as evidence of good effort. Continue working on your craft to help you stand out even among your toughest peers.

to shuffle slowly to the C Roster. He glanced over his shoulder. Sam watched with a blank expression, but his eyes gave away his thoughts. George turned away from the pity he saw shining there.

He heard a low moan. Anthony Snoodlecone was frantically searching the C Roster and apparently coming up blank. A teacher whispered to him. Looked like Anthony hadn't made it at all. The only thing worse than being a C Roster student was being an RPC. Some villains joked that, instead of Regular *Public* Citizen, "RPC" stood for Really *Pathetic* Citizen.

But maybe C Roster was even worse than getting cut completely. Maybe it would be better to go home now than to live among the A Roster kids and know he'd be one of the villains taking their falls for them and joked about by the RPC media, who didn't even know the difference between a villain and the garden-variety burglars in the police reels of *Bloopers by Dumb Criminals*. Hadn't he spent the last several years laughing at them too? To be one of them would be humiliating. Maybe Anthony was luckier than he knew.

George's legs trembled as he walked forward. He didn't have to elbow anyone aside here. The group of fifteen students stood there like RPCs in a stickup, jaws slack with shock. Horror rose on a few of their faces.

Quickly, George looked down the short list of names. He swallowed. There it was. George Pruwell. A stupid C Roster villain.

Bile coated the back of his throat, but he clamped his lips on the vomit that threatened to spew and swallowed it back down. Humiliation spattered him like pigeon poo on the sidewalk. His fingers and toes felt numb. There was no Distinguished Villain plaque in his future now.

Should he quit? He imagined showing back up at his house, telling his mom. He bit back a groan and imagined facing Alex. The thought alone made George blanch.

No, he couldn't leave the Academy. Not yet. They'd made a mistake. He belonged here. Villainy was his life, his whole family's life. He might be C Roster for now, but he'd find a way out of this.

He looked at the frightened, sad eyes of his peer group and stood straighter. He didn't belong with them, no matter what mistakes he'd made in the past. Maybe C Roster was the best *they* could hope for, but not him. He was a Pruwell villain, dang it! There was nothing good about the Pruwells. And he'd prove it.

CHAPTER 11
THE WRONG ROSTER

THE NEXT MORNING at breakfast, George realized that being a member of C Roster had its benefits. He got to eat dried prunes for the first time in his life. True, the prunes helped the kids deal with the inevitable constipation that came with the unhappy stress of being in the lowest roster, but the dried fruit tasted sweeter than anything he'd had before. That was nothing to sneeze at.

The school probably figured C Roster kids weren't valuable enough to worry about corrupting with sweetness anyway. They just weren't evil enough to maintain their edge. They didn't even have an edge, so the rules were a little more lax for them. Turning down cookies at Daniel's would have been a lot more difficult if George had known what he'd been missing.

He also got his new official dorm room assignment. He worried about what his roommate would be like.

Probably a C Roster too. He heaved a sigh.

After taking the elevator to the third floor, he walked into his new room. Spartan-like, it had two beds, two dressers, and two closets in a space the size of a peanut. Sam was unpacking on the left side. "Wait, what are you doing here?" George sputtered.

"A Rosters get to pick their roommates," Sam said, shrugging. He hung up another black trench coat. He seemed to have a collection of them.

Shocked, George had to ask, "Uh, why would you want to room with me? I mean, you're A list, and I'm…"

He couldn't finish the sentence.

Sam clearly knew what George meant and shrugged again, turning away as if putting away every article of clothing was the most important assignment of his life. "You know, 'cause you won't try to kill me in my sleep. You don't have it in you to get rid of the competition that way."

George gulped. He wondered if anyone would be so cold as to kill him just to improve their odds.

"Don't worry," Sam said, seeming to read his mind. "I mean, you're a C Roster, so… " He trailed off, turning red.

"So no one will bother to kill me?" George finished,

his voice raising a little.

Sam shrugged. "Look, you just helped people too much. It makes the chancellors suspicious that you won't ever be evil enough, you know?"

"What about you?" sulked George, kicking at the carpet a little. "You've been nice to me!"

Sam walked to the doorway, checked the hall, and then closed the door. He whispered, "Yeah, but I'm careful about letting them see it. Like, I didn't say we were friends. I told them you'd be a good sidekick one day."

Mixed emotions flooded George. Insult at the idea of being a sidekick mingled painfully with Sam's declaration of friendship.

Sam continued. "No one in the A Roster talks, so I look just as unfriendly as the rest there. *And* I have a talent for sorcery, so I can get away with a little more. I'm a rare find. But you? You're going to have to really kick it up a notch. You're going to have to do something really spectacular to get their attention and change your roster assignment."

Hope swelled in George. "You really think that's even possible?"

Sam grinned. "Sure. You're the brother of Alexander

the Terrible, after all!"

George's smile flickered out, but before Sam could ask why, George said, "Let's get to class. I don't want to be late on my first day."

He wondered if Sam just wanted to be friends with the brother of the most famous villain of recent years. Why else would anyone want to hang out with George? The thought hurt like a Poison Dart 3000X numbing his face, numbing his heart.

Serena was already in the elevator when they stepped in, her big brown eyes sparkling. "Time for class, boys!"

George sullenly shifted his book bag to his other shoulder. "You sure seem chipper and ready to go for someone in C Roster."

"Well, I figure it's better than getting kicked out. I try to make the best of things." She flashed her pearly whites, which was probably why she was in C Roster in the first place, especially with an optimistic attitude like that. It was like she wasn't even trying.

Geez Louise, had no one ever taught her anything? Unless she was willing and able to stab someone in the back right after offering that smile, a glowing grin was only a liability in this school.

Serena chatted about which brand of cape she wanted to buy when she had saved up enough. George stared at his reflection in the mirror of the elevator. He didn't even have to remind himself to scowl.

Serena and George hurried off to their classroom for a day full of boring lessons taught by Chancellor Tuttle. *With a boring name like that, no wonder he teaches the C Roster*, thought George. Before the professor arrived, George had his pen and paper ready, his textbook open to *The Secrets to Stellar Safecracking*. He'd already read this last year at home, but it never hurt to be ahead of the game, even in C Roster.

By midday, though, he sort of wished he hadn't read ahead. At least he wouldn't have been bored out of his mind all morning. Plus, was there any torture worse than listening to one eleven-year-old after another read out loud from the textbook, voices breaking from nerves? George didn't think so.

Then they walked into a long room lined with safes, from easiest to most difficult to crack. They all had to stand around while Tuttle pointed out the obvious features of the thing, his bald head shining in the glaring overhead lights.

"This is the safe door. This is the safe's body. Here is the lock mechanism, class."

George had proven he could break into any safe during Trial Week, but here he was again, stuck with kids who couldn't. Just because he was too nice. He gritted his teeth, watching every other student in his class stare in bafflement at what was *clearly* a Model 7Z Lock Manifesto, not even a hard safe to crack. It was as easy as peeling an onion.

Like the safecracking lesson, the rest of the day passed slowly. His lab partner in poison class, Eugene Festoobin, nearly fed them Wart Face poison by confusing it with the distinctive cup of antidote sitting beside it. Luckily, George swapped them at the last moment. He rolled his eyes so hard they nearly fell out of his head. The teachers thought he belonged with *this* group?

Classes met from 6:00 a.m. to 6:00 p.m. George felt like he was stuck in molasses as the school week went by, day by agonizing day.

Notetaking, test taking, practicing a few simple skills he already had, but very little villainy or wrongdoing actually took place. This wasn't what he had imagined at all.

His schedule was:

8-9 Safecracking and Lockpicking 101

9-10 Social Networking: Choose Your Villain Name and Promote It

10-11 Poisons, Natural and Artificial

12-2 Lunch and Alone Time to Practice Sullen Glowering

2-3 Selecting Your Villain to Support

3-4 Evil Laughter and Other Trappings

4-5 Life as a Sidekick, Modified

Each lesson left him less and less satisfied. He knew all this. He had studied hard before coming here. He owned the most recent edition of *The All-Inclusive Encyclopedia of Superheroes* and could recite every name in there and list what each hero's power was. He had grown his own garden full of poisonous plants and only made himself sick twice. He'd come here to learn to be a real villain, not to take notes on stuff he'd already studied.

He glared, not even needing a mirror to know he practically had laser beams flashing from his eyes. Insulting, that's what this was. Serena had been wrong: C Roster was worse than not being here at the Academy at all. He'd have to show them how evil he could really be.

How tough. How darn scary.

At the end of their first week in their new placements, George finally reached his boiling point during Life as a Sidekick[13] class. Their teacher said, "Of course, being C Roster, only half of you will end up being as skilled as even petty criminals. The lucky ones among you will end up as sidekicks, so please keep that in mind while we study how villains select their sidekicks. If you must be a sidekick, our training will help you to know how to find a high-level villain. Better to be a sidekick to a Distinguished Villain, in many cases, than be a piddly villain on your own who never gets the chance to perform any real crimes at all, right?"

Chancellor Tuttle snorted a loud laugh, which echoed in the silent room. Fourteen pairs of eyes looked at him with heartbreak. But George looked at him full of rage. The teacher met George's fiery gaze and nodded. "See

---

13   Sidekick: "A partner of lesser power (and stature) who assists in crime or, for a hero, assists in the unfair assault of a hardworking villain. In either case, sidekicks are treated with respect, but a certain condescension is required to maintain proper authority between leader and sidekick. Some villains' sidekicks are incorrectly called "henchmen," by RPC.s, but please note that henchmen are actually a higher level of trust and responsibility, often sent on unsupervised errands for their boss. See H for henchmen, pg. 134." From A Villain's Dictionary

me after class, George."

After the bell rang, George tried to cling to his anger. He'd felt so good then. He felt big and brave and… villainous. And now it was slipping away, leaving the same old polite, nice, boring George who had gotten himself stuck in C Roster in the first place.

"So, George, how do you like your classes?" Chancellor Tuttle asked, a lilt in his voice. It reminded George that while this man may be teaching C Roster, he was a graduate from this school, and not C Roster, either. Only A Rosters came back to teach. George wasn't sure why Tuttle was teaching this level, though. Maybe he'd made somebody angry.

George knew this was his moment. It was now or never. He cleared his throat, wishing for Voice Amplifier JuiceTM, and said, "They're boring." The moment dragged out. He added, because he couldn't help himself, "If you don't mind me saying, sir."

Tuttle shook his head. "George, *George*. I know there's some heat in there, some strength that could be put to good use. I've seen glimpses of it. You were brave to rescue that girl, even if misguided. That took guts, though, and villains need guts. But those small acts of kindness to your classmates when you thought the teachers weren't looking? Those did you in. I argued to put you in B Roster because you did well in many of the trials, but the rest of the team thought you were just too… nice." He winced as he said the word.

George winced too.

Tuttle continued. "But I did get a concession. The school is putting out an open call soon to attack a highly prized superhero. We do that now and then. The student who takes the assignment will gain huge points in the eyes of the chancellors. Normally, only A and B students can take a job like that, but I got permission to let you try for it too. The others in C Roster need to move slower than you, and it's irritating, frankly, to have you always knowing the answers."

George couldn't quite get past the phrase *attack a highly prized superhero.*

"George." Tuttle snapped his fingers. "George, do you hear what I'm saying? And the student who beats the superhero is *guaranteed* a slot in A Roster for their entire time at the Academy."

George gasped.

Tuttle continued, "Yes, you heard correctly. A Roster. Choice of dorm room. Top assignment after graduation. And for this particular assignment, we might be able to arrange for a Distinguished Villain plaque to be awarded despite student status—a first in the history of our school."

George smiled. A slow, evil smile. His mother would have been proud.

Tuttle warned, "When the call goes out, you'll need to be first in line. They're not considering anyone's skills, mind you. Just willingness to tackle the problem."

George asked, "And who's the... *problem?*"

Tuttle shook his head. "I'm not allowed to tell. No one is. You've got to find out with everyone else right when they open up the offer. But I can tell you this is your chance, kid. Take it, or you'll be C Roster until you graduate and end up flipping burgers and stealing customers' change at the register, know what I mean?"

George did.

CHAPTER 12

THE PROBLEM

BACK IN THEIR dorm room, George told Sam everything Tuttle had said.

"Why would he set you up like that?" Sam asked. His eyebrows formed a dark V.

George looked at his friend with surprise. "What do you mean? He's trying to help."

Sam rolled his eyes. "George, this isn't *superhero* school. We're the bad guys. Why try to help a kid from C Roster make A Roster or get a Distinguished Villain plaque?"

George shrugged, trying to pretend he didn't care, but his hurt feelings shoved words in his mouth he wouldn't usually say. "Okay, if villains never help anyone, then why are *you* trying to help me? Just to network with my brother?"

He jutted out his jaw, embarrassment tangling with fear.

Sam laughed. "Pu-leeze, George. I like hanging out with you, all right? You know lots of stuff. Plus, you crack me up. Now, chill out, you nut."

George flushed with surprised pleasure. Sam really did consider him a friend.

Sam continued, bringing George back to the point. "Look, I just don't want you to get killed. What if you go up against some big superhero at this stage in the game? You can barely fly straight, even in the new capes! You're awesome with machines and explosives, sure, but what if the superhero is one of those guys who's been around a thousand years and lives without any electronics? You'd be toast, my man."

George gritted his teeth. Sam made sense, but he didn't understand the importance of this last chance to get into A Roster. George hadn't called home to tell his family what his roster assignment was. Not yet.

He'd kept postponing, thinking he'd wait until he got used to it, but time was running out. Student roster assignments were supposed to be top secret, to protect the A Roster kids from getting taken out, but everyone in the school knew, and what everyone here knew, *everyone* in the villain world would soon know.

George's mother would die of shame to have a C

Roster kid. His brother had made A Roster. Now it was George's turn. If he took this assignment, he would have a chance to redeem himself.

He took out his lucky quarter. The tiny grooves along the edges were rough on his fingers. George looked at the coin intently before flipping it in the air, catching it, and then slapping it onto the back of his hand.

A second later, he tossed the coin on his nightstand without looking at the results. Whether it was heads or tails didn't matter. He had to do this.

The next morning after assembly, A Roster instructor Chancellor Brillow announced, "All A and B Roster students stay for an open call. C Roster is dismissed." The rest of George's peers began to file out of the assembly hall like lemmings headed for their personal cliffs.

George stood there, feeling awkward, until Tuttle leaned over and whispered to Chancellor Brillow. She sighed and added, "George Pruwell may stay as well."

This earned him several speculative looks, but George didn't care. He was sliding up the side rows. He wanted to be the very first in line. If he took the golden paper of assignment first, he was... well, golden.

Sam slipped up behind him. "Still gonna go through with it?"

George only nodded. Sam clapped him once on the shoulder, which was as close as he could get to wishing George luck in front of all these people. But it helped. That one kind gesture soothed the wild moths in his stomach.

When Chancellor Brillow began reading, George was already racing up to accept the assignment. He didn't even notice that not a single other soul was moving forward until he was holding the golden paper, having whipped it from her hand.

Her voice trailed off. "Are you certain, George?"

George nodded, a broad smile across his face. He'd done it! He had a chance now. He'd show them!

Everyone stared at him with eyes the size of Forbidden Fruit.[14]

---

14   From *Shortcuts for Villains Short-on-Time*: Instead of brewing a Sleep potion, which could take weeks, simply buy Forbidden Fruit from Villain Vittles! They've already done the necessary work and injected it into large, ripe apples. Simply hand the fruit to your victim, tell him he must not eat a single bite, and then leave the room. His snores will tell you when the coast is clear. Provides six hours of steady Zs, perfect for liberating large pieces of furniture from their abode. Nectarines can be substituted for apples upon request.

It slowly occurred to him that surely at least one other student should have charged forward too. Chancellor Brillow's face was chalky.

George looked down at the paper, smoothing it unconsciously with his hands. The words swam for a moment before he could make out the sentence.

Attack and defeat Captain Perfectus,
Superhero of the Ages.

The words of the chancellor were tinny and far away. "George? George? Talk to me!"

The words spilled from George's lips even while his brain screamed at him. "I accept. I will defeat Captain Perfectus."

Captain Perfectus was only the most powerful superhero ever to live. He had defeated whole hosts of villains without breaking a sweat. George didn't think Captain Perfectus ever sweated.

There was no way one lone villain-in-training—C Roster, no less—could defeat such a foe. But the decision was made. For George, he'd rather go down fighting a superhero than go out not trying at all. It was the way he'd always figured he'd end his career. He just hadn't expected to reach the end before he'd even begun.

The assignment came with a few directions, at least. Chancellor Brillow took George aside to give him the rest of the information. "Perfectus has recently arrived in our city and moved into the Plaza Hotel, which is far too close to our school for safety. He shows signs of living there permanently, which cannot be allowed. We must not be discovered by any superhero, but we suspect he may know our location. He must be removed, by any means necessary. You have three days before the professional team will be assembled. But we prefer to not pay for—I mean, to not wait for them. Anything could happen in three days. This is your chance to move up in the world by showing yourself worthy. Do you understand?"

George did. He just wasn't sure he was worthy enough for this task. In fact, he was pretty sure he wasn't, but he was going to do his best anyway. It's what his dad would expect. And some small part of George, a very tiny hopeful part, whispered, *But wouldn't it be amazing if this did work?*

As soon as George reached his empty room, he

jumped online and searched for the Plaza Hotel, New York. Their webpage looked swanky, with the golden backward and forward P of the Plaza logo. Classical violins and cellos played a short, soft tune.

George thought for a moment. He clicked on *Reservations*. He filled in the *check availability* search function to get an idea if there were any rooms open for tomorrow at all. If so, those would be off his list of potential rooms for Perfectus. George gaped at the images of the hotel. Everything looked really fancy.

"What are you looking at?" Sam asked, locking the door behind him.

George was so startled that he nearly fell off the chair. He hadn't even noticed when Sam had come in. *Keen villain awareness.* George sighed at himself.

"The Plaza," he said, gesturing to the screen. "That's where Perfectus is staying. Superhero gigs must pay well!"

Sam frowned. "You're still really going to try this? The whole school's talking about how impossible this assignment is."

George gave a firm nod. "I've got to."

Sam gazed out the window for a long moment. Then he shrugged once and turned back to George. "Okay, tell me what you've found out so far. The least I can do is help you not get killed, my dude."

Gratitude and relief tightened George's throat, so he cleared it gruffly and waved Sam over, trying to look casual, though he felt anything but.

The boys looked over the descriptions of each room, eyes nearly popping out at the luxury described.

Sam said, "And, dude, look at these views!"

Excitement began to grow in George as he stared at the room images. "Perfectus could be sitting in a room just like that one at this very moment."

"Sure, but he could be in any of them. Well, the school wouldn't be trying to get rid of him if he were just hanging out for a week anyway. We should see if we could find out which rooms are for long-term residents. It might cut down the search some." Sam sprawled on his bed.

He had a point. The Plaza was big. George hadn't realized how big it was until now.

"He's *somewhere* in there." George groaned. "But finding him feels impossible!" He heard the whining tone creep into his voice but felt helpless to stop it.

Sam flicked his hair out of his face and said, "What we need is some more intel. First things first. Rule number one from *Plotting Evil Schemes*[15], remember? What does any self-respecting villain do before he sets down plans for a heist?"

George began to smile. "Go undercover to case the joint."

Sam replied, "Yep, and this is just another kind of heist. Think of it that way." He sat up and hesitated a moment before adding, "But, George, what if the school *is* setting you up? Are you sure you trust this info about the Plaza? How do we even know he's really there?"

Good point. George wanted to slap his forehead again. There he went, being too trusting again. Maybe this *was* the test, to see if he could see through their scam. So they'd go check things out. He was glad to not be alone.

---

15 *Plotting Evil Schemes*: The personal manifesto and autobiography of esteemed villain, Allegra Maestra, who stole over two hundred grand pianos from upscale piano shops during her career. However, she's most well-known for successfully and diabolically introducing soft jazz into the world of music.

CHAPTER 13

THE GROUNDWORK

GEORGE FELT RIDICULOUS in green-and-pink Bermuda shorts and a T-shirt that read *I Love New York*. He tugged on his shirt, complaining to Sam, "I look like a goofball."

"Don't be dumb," Sam scolded. "You're *supposed* to look like a goofball. You're supposed to be a tourist."

"Why can't I look like your kind of tourist?" George eyed Sam's dark jeans and white tee.

"We can't look like twins. Besides, I pull this look off better." Sam swished his hair back with a grin.

Unfortunately, George had to admit this was true. So he got to be the goofy tourist.

"Okay, but we're going to walk down to the Plaza without wasting time. No visit to Central Park, no trip to the zoo, no tourist traps, got it?"

Sam saluted. "Yes, sir!"

George laughed, and the boys slipped down the hall.

Outside, the birds sang, oblivious to George's racing pulse. The tall buildings seemed like a prison this time around, more terrifying than beautiful. By the time the two of them reached the hotel, George's tongue stuck to the roof of his mouth from sheer nerves.

The Plaza Hotel sat smug among the giant skyscrapers that towered over it but would never be as famous. Why on earth would a superhero stay at such a prestigious, obvious location? Wasn't he supposed to live far from crowds, in order to protect the innocents who might perish in a mighty battle with a villain? George shrugged. No guessing the mind of the greatest superhero to live in ages.

Walking into the lobby didn't help his nerves. A soaring ceiling and walls that glinted gold took what little breath he had left. Crystal chandeliers hung like frozen snowflakes. Men and women glided by dressed in dark dresses and suits. George stuck out like a flamingo in a pack of penguins. "Uh, maybe this wasn't a good idea."

Sam stopped and lifted the shades he had decided to sport. "Look. You want to get him, right?"

George gulped. "Yeah."

"Well, this is part of it. You're either in or you're not. Which is it?"

George looked at the elegance around him. He never quite seemed to fit in anywhere he went, but this was worse than usual.

Sam whispered, "My family's stayed at places a lot like this, okay? Not in the best room or anything, but you're just as cool as anyone I met at any of those fancy hotels."

George didn't know what to say. His family mostly lived on his dad's Villainy Prison Insurance[16], though George's mom worked part-time at a villain department store when she wasn't homeschooling him. Neither provided much extra for vacations or hotels.

This was ridiculous. What was he thinking? Someone like Sam should've gotten this assignment: A Roster, used to wealth and elegance. Look at their chosen villain outfits, for crying out loud. What kind of villain chose flaming tights?

George was about to turn and leave when he heard the concierge say, "Of course, sir. We'll send someone up

---

16   Villainy Prison Insurance: Living the life of a villain is fraught with risk. Will you endanger your family by cutting off their income if you ever end up in the clink? Through your monthly insurance premiums, Villainy Prison Insurance promises to care for your family during your unfortunate incarceration experience.

to fix the new cracks in the floor immediately. It might help, sir, if you tried to tiptoe. Yes, sir, I realize you are not a ballet dancer, but someone such as... yourself... can easily damage flooring just by walking."

George lost his breath with a *whoosh*. A sudden realization sent tingles across his whole body. He turned to Sam. "Who do we know who could crack the floors just by walking?"

Sam nodded with the fierce smile of a pro-gamer locking on to the final boss.

Confirmation received—this was no hoax. George was really going to go up against Perfectus, because the superhero was here. It had to be him.

The boys scurried back out the door into the bright sunlight. The intelligence from the school was right. Now George just needed to figure out where exactly in the Plaza to find his target.

George was still no good at hacking into databases. But he knew someone who was. Derek Smiley knew more about computer hacking than any other student. He was A Roster, like Sam. Though George had only given Derek that extra pencil one day during Trial Week, Derek seemed to find it very uncomfortable to owe even such a small favor as that. He'd avoided George as much as possible since then.

Sam approached him during class and quietly asked for some assistance. Derek was always ready for a challenge and thankful to discharge his debt. He got them into the Plaza's database in no time.

"No one here by the name of Perfectus," he said, shaking his head.

George chewed his lip. "Can you see which rooms are available?"

"Easy," Derek said. He pulled up a floor plan of the hotel. Looking at the rooms in use, George could see almost every room was taken. That didn't help much.

"All I can do is this," Derek finally said, handing George a few papers. "These are the different floor plans of the rooms. If you can figure out which type of room he's in, at least you'll know how to get around in it during the fight."

George's stomach shrank. *The fight*. As he took the papers, they almost slid from his hand. It reminded him of the first day of tryouts. He stood a bit straighter. "Thanks a lot, Derek. And Sam. I appreciate your help."

Derek shrugged. "I think it's uncool to send a kid out to do a grown villain's job, you know?"

George flushed. "It's okay. I want to do it."

Derek shrugged again. "It's your life. For now, anyway."

George's shoulders prickled with embarrassment as Derek left.

Sam said, "Don't worry about him. You know how to figure things out with logic, like the maze thing. You can do this."

George was glad someone believed in him, since he wasn't sure he believed in himself. He might even find Perfectus, but defeat him? George buried his face in his pillow. He never had been very good at lying, especially not to himself. Before he left, he knew he needed to make a call.

"Mom?" George said, softly.

"Oh, honey," she replied, her voice thick with tears. "Melinda Rogue, the guidance counselor from the school, gave me a call. She said you accepted a very dangerous assignment. Why? Dad is already in prison for the rest of his life—and he was the top of his field! I thought for sure you'd choose a sensible villainy path like Alex did, where you wouldn't actually *fight* a superhero."

His mother's clear belief that he would certainly fail took the last bit of his hope. "I know. But you don't want me to be C Roster, do you?"

There was a long silence. "You're... C Roster?"

Sweat broke out across his brow. "That's why I'm taking this job." He swallowed loudly. "I thought you knew?"

She sighed. "No, but it all makes sense now. George, I'm sure there's tutoring available, right? I know you work so hard!"

"No, Mom, this is my only chance to move out of C Roster." Disappointing her felt worse than he'd thought it would.

Silence. Most unusual for his mother. Then she said, "C Roster isn't the worst thing in life. And, honey... if you want to come home, we'll figure something out. What do *you* want to do?"

George hesitated a long moment, shocked. His mother never asked questions like that unless she really meant for him to answer them. "I want to make our family proud. I want to be A Roster and a Distinguished Villain one day."

His mother seemed to struggle with words. "I... George, I want you to know that—"

Suddenly, Alex was speaking on the phone, with their mom sniffling in the background. "Well, well, little bro. You're the one they got to go after Perfectus?"

George nodded and then realized his brother couldn't see. "Uh, yeah."

"You still got your coin?"

George smiled, his heart lifting slightly. "Of course!"

"Promise me you'll take it with you, okay?"

"I promise."

"Go for it, little bro. You've got to go for it, or you'll always wonder what would've happened."

Alex made sense. This was George's life's goal, right? Better to try and fail than not try at all. That's what his mother always told him. Even if he didn't beat Captain Perfectus, maybe the school would at least be impressed with his guts and move him in B Roster. Well, that is if Perfectus didn't wrap him into a burrito and send him to the state prison instead.

"Thanks, Alex. I'm going for it, and I'll have my coin with me."

"Perfect," Alex replied. "Or should I say, *Perfectus*?

Now, go get some good sleep, little bro."

George didn't think he'd be able to sleep, but with his brother's unexpected encouragement, he drifted off.

The next morning, it was time to go. Today was day two before the pros would come in on day three, taking away his chance to win his rightful spot at the school.

He couldn't eat. The school had provided an all-black jumpsuit for him, perhaps out of pity, but in a fit of defiance, he put on his flame tights costume. He didn't have much to take with him. He'd been saving money for a new ray gun, for now he only had Alex's first hand-me-down gun.

George stared at himself in the mirror. Any and all optimism gained from his brother's pep talk popped like a soap bubble. George couldn't deny the truth. He was short, weak, and seriously goofy. He had no super-tools except his one pathetic ray gun. It probably couldn't even burn a hole through an aluminum can. His chest felt as empty as his tool belt.

Sam walked up alongside him, holding something. "Take this," he urged. "You'll need it."

He pressed his black leather trench coat into George's hands. "You'll need to look like a serious villain.

Plus, this leather is coated with a special anti-heat chemical that keeps you cool even in hot situations."

The leather felt softer than the liver pâté his mother served spread on spinach crackers.

Sam continued. "And this. I won't need it until next semester." He placed a Tool of All Occasions[17] on top of the coat.

Normally, George would have drooled and inspected the tool. He'd wanted one for ages but could never have afforded it. Right now, though, he just buckled it onto one loop of his belt and then struck a pose, showing off his outfit.

"If I'm going to go down in flames, might as well look the part," he joked.

Sam whistled as he shook his head in awe. "I had no idea you had nerves of steel. You might do this thing yet."

George didn't bother explaining it wasn't nerves

---

17   Tool of All Occasions: From the magazine *Such a Bargain, It's a Crime*: "This spectacular tool gives you an amazing advantage over any foe. Screwdriver, hammer, pliers, knife, and can opener on one side. Electric jack, magnet, clippers, and extension cord hidden in the other. The body of the tool functions as a homing device, a cell phone, and a music player for those times when you need to kick back after a hard day's work robbing banks or pursuing world domination."

of steel. He'd simply accepted his own defeat. Villain kids weren't put in juvie these days—they always broke out of it too easily. So, he could very possibly end up as the youngest prison inmate ever. Heck, there was some notoriety in that, at least.

A giggle nearly escaped his lips, but he pushed it back. No need to scare the nice roommate who was handing over his very expensive equipment. "Thanks, Sam."

There was a knock on the door. George considered leaping over the bed in a single bound but just couldn't muster the energy. He walked over to it instead and opened the door.

On the other side stood Elizabeth Shade, red hair wild around her flushed face. "Here," she blurted out, thrusting her fist forward. "This is for helping me when I got trapped in the maze. I know that probably got you stuck in C Roster."

She pushed a watch into his hand. The large faceplate glowed a soft orange. Several other dials and tiny screens flickered along the edges.

"It's a Hero Detector," Elizabeth explained. "Whenever you're in range of a superhero, it'll turn black. It'll also let you know your own vital statistics, like your heart rate—" She cut herself off, looking like she'd just swallowed a large diamond to sneak past security. Elizabeth then raised her arms like she might give an awkward hug but froze, offered a half wave, and then fled down the hall.

George stared after her in surprise. He'd never imagined real villains could actually have friends, certainly not more than one. Bad for business, after all. Daniel had only gotten as close as he had because he lived right down the street, and he didn't even know the truth about George's family. No RPC could. And none of the villain co-op kids had ever bothered to get to know him.

But here, Sam and Elizabeth were both... friends. George rolled the word around in his mouth, savoring it like a sweet prune. *Friends.*

He had just shut the door when another C Roster student knocked. This time, it was Christina Pinkles. She stood shifting her weight between her feet as if she might take off running any second.

He'd told her when a big assignment's due date had been moved forward. She'd been in the bathroom at the time and would've failed if she'd turned it in late. She was always missing deadlines and losing stuff as it was, which was clearly the only reason why she was in C Roster, given how brilliant she was. A sidekick would make up for her disorganization and help her genius shine—their teachers should've seen that. George didn't feel like she owed him anything. She obviously felt differently.

She handed him what appeared to be a ballpoint pen. "When you're ready to take him out," she said, looking nervously up and down the hall, "push this button here, and a knife will pop out." She pointed to a tiny blue button at the top of the pen. "It's made of titanium steel, so it's hard enough to cut through anything, even Captain Perfectus, if you end up needing to. But watch out—the knife comes out fast."

She wasn't joking. George nearly stabbed himself when he grazed the button and a six-inch blade flew out of the tip. "How'd that fit in there?"

A ghost of a smile flitted across her face. "That's my little secret."

George didn't think he could ever stab someone, but he smiled back at her. "This is really good. You'll make a great criminal mastermind one day."

She blushed and took her leave quickly.

George didn't care about giving compliments and encouragement anymore. What was the worst they could do to him? Ruin his career? Oh, wait, he'd already done that to himself. He snorted, closing the door. This time, it stayed shut until morning. Until it was time. Time to go face Captain Perfectus.

CHAPTER 14

THE JOURNEY

GEORGE HAD SAID his goodbyes. He had memorized the various floor plans of the Plaza. He had gathered his tools, which consisted of one hand-me-down ray-gun from Alex and those items George's classmates had shared, at risk to their own careers. Even so, his tool belt still looked pathetically empty, so he added a couple of fake grenades from the Unusually Dangerous Weapons to Own extra-credit seminar.

Studying the final results in the full-length closet mirror, George decided he looked vaguely carsick. He added a scowl. There. He looked more like he meant business.

With a sharp nod to himself, he slipped his brother's lucky coin into his shoe, double-checked the harness of his ray gun, and re-cinched his tool belt. Eventually, there was nothing left to do but go find Captain Perfectus.

It was time for action.

George stepped out of the Academy into the busy

New York sidewalk and squinted against the sunlight. He'd forgotten a cool pair of shades. Of course he had. Oh well.

He took a minute to let his eyes adjust. People flooded past him. He felt like a minnow caught up in a stream of businesspeople and joggers. The tiny screen on Elizabeth's nifty Hero-Detector watch informed him that his heart had sped up to a hundred and fifty-two beats per minute, and the soft orange glow indicated no superhero was nearby. George took a deep breath. Well, he knew where to go to find one of those.

He only took two steps before he got banged on the shoulder by a passing RPC the size of a giant. Two more adults pushed past, shoving George farther down the street. Being short for his age meant he couldn't see over the heads of the people around him, but it also meant it would be easy to hide, he realized. The long black trench coat covered his costume. Villains didn't announce themselves until they had the upper hand, or at least were in position. Villainy 101. He could do this part, at least.

For the first time this morning, a smile crossed George's face. He slipped in and out of the crowd. *I'm like a little snake slithering through the grass*, he thought to himself. Perhaps George the Duck had become George the Snake… or maybe George the Lizard, no, wait, George the Komodo Dragon. Yeah, that was even better.

George was so busy thinking of exciting villain titles that he stepped into the street without noticing the red flashing-hand sign. A car blared as it zipped by two inches from him, but he managed to yank himself back to the curb without getting run over.

Ugh, already making mistakes! Well, he would totally keep his head in the game from now on. No more daydreaming. *Just be villainous*, he reminded himself.

Slinking down the sidewalks of New York City, George wished he had time to eat the simmering hot dogs that scented the air. He hadn't eaten one here yet. Boiled hot dogs were not only acceptable villainy food, they were also good to force-feed healthy superheroes while keeping them hostage. Those health nuts really freaked out about them[18]. George grinned but then caught himself. *Be villainous!*

---

18   From *Know Thy Enemy*: "Superheroes enjoy such foods as grilled chicken breasts, raw spinach salads, fruit smoothies, kale chips, boiled eggs, and brown rice. If taken hostage, they should on no account be allowed to eat any of these foods. Instead, offer them only Wonder Bread bologna sandwiches, boiled hot dogs, syrupy pancakes, and soda. In other words, if it is a favorite food of a typical American RPC. child, it's a good torture food for superheroes. The one exception to this is Cheerios, which toddlers and superheroes alike adore. Avoid these."

He glared around at the slew of people who never bothered to look down at him. He wondered what they would think if they knew a superhero would soon be battling a villain right near them. Maybe they'd be excited, but they might just as easily be frightened.

It wasn't like these innocents were in danger anyway. He was in a lot more danger than anyone else near the hotel. With a resigned sigh, George pulled his trench coat a little tighter. He stepped past the golden statue of the fountain, noticing the way the light reflected off the surface, a dancing shimmer. He lingered a moment to enjoy the view, feeling rather rebellious as he did so.

He paused for a moment longer while a horse-drawn carriage clopped by. As the dark-brown horse passed, George quickly reached out and gave it a gentle pat. Its coat was so soft. The horse whickered softly. George felt his chest loosen a little bit.

Crossing the street wasn't too bad. As he stepped into the blast of air conditioning inside the hotel for the second time in his life, he hoped it wouldn't be his last.

The lobby was full of quick-stepping people wrapped in bland business suits and pastel sweaters. The black leather trench coat down to his ankles stood out here like a red cape with a big S would stand out at the Academy. His goal wasn't to fit in anymore, but to clearly be a villain. If he was only going to get this one shot at it, he wanted to embrace his villainy while he could. Still, he found himself slinking rather than strutting, hoping he wouldn't trip.

He checked his watch. Still glowing orange. *If I were a superhero in this building, where would I stay?* How would George know where to go? Then he smiled because the answer clicked into his mind the way logic puzzle answers often did. Suddenly, it was obvious.

Inside the elevator, he pressed the button for the twentieth floor. If you could fly, why would you bother with the elevators when you could just swoop in and land on the open terrace of a penthouse suite? The elevator rose with a speed that sent his stomach lurching.

Sure enough, right as the elevator reached the twentieth floor, his watch faded to dark gray. George licked his lips. Showtime. Nerves rattled through his body like a bucket of nails in the dryer, shaking his knees.

Maybe he'd get really lucky and fight Perfectus to a standstill in some amazing fashion. George let himself imagine it for a second, the possibility of *any* kind of victory, but then the elevator dinged, announcing the doors were about to open. His daydream of victory vanished. He pulled out his ray gun and took careful aim. His hands were shaking, but Perfectus would be a pretty big target at this range. Hard for even George to miss.

No need for fancy entrances or sneaky attacks, not this time. George figured the most he could hope for was to at least singe the guy.

He tightened the grip of his ray gun. This wasn't just any ray gun, either, not anymore. He'd stayed up late last night, calibrating the light containment device to ensure maximum power. This ray gun could take down the side of the building now. But it probably still wouldn't take down Captain Perfectus. He was called perfect for a reason, after all.

The doors slid open. George had to take a deep breath to keep from hitting the *close doors* button. Was jail or even death really preferable to C Roster status?

He thought for a long moment. Yes. Yes, it was.

He slipped out of the trench coat, taking the time to fold it and set it next to the elevator. The orange flames crawling up his arms and legs would pronounce him clearly as a villain to Perfectus. Today, George *was* a villain, if only for this once. He stepped out of the elevator to face his future. Hopefully, he still had one.

CHAPTER 15

THE CONFRONTATION

THE DOORS SLID closed behind George, abandoning him to his fate. Beyond the elevators, the room doors looked identical. He glanced at his watch for guidance.

Lifting it toward his left, he saw light flickers of orange. But to his right, it darkened until he could barely read the hands on the clock or see his pulse and blood pressure. He really wished there was a way to turn those numbers off anyway.

George set off to his right and continued down the hall, lifting his arm next to each door until he reached the final suite at the end of the long hallway. His watch went so black that he couldn't see the numbers of his racing pulse at all.

However, even without the watch, he'd have known this was the suite. A steel portcullis covered the entire door, from ceiling to floor, anchored by a sophisticated lock that George recognized from his safecracking course. He licked his lips as he leaned closer. Just looking at the familiar mechanism made him calmer. Yes, this was a LockPro 5000[19], top of the line. Naturally, a superhero like Captain Perfectus would be able to afford it.

Sliding the ray gun into its hip holster, George examined the portcullis that blocked the door. He couldn't even knock through the interlocking bars that blocked the ordinary hotel door behind it. He thought for a long moment, running through the possibilities from what he knew of this particular model. Then he smiled.

He pulled out Sam's Tool of All Occasions and looked through the different compartments along its slender length. The thing weighed nearly five pounds because it packed a lot of tools in such a small space. Finally, he found what he was looking for: a tiny amplification device that he carefully placed against the lock.

An electric sizzle hit his ears a split second before a sharp shock sent him flying backward into the wall.

---

19   LockPro's TV ad—"Your One-Stop-Shop for every security need. From cape locks to alarm systems that will pack up the trespasser for you and ship 'em to the nearest Big House, LockPro knows that heroes and villains have a higher need for privacy than the average human. You aren't average. Why should your locks be?"

Thankful that the pain had only lasted a second, George gasped, blinking hard. The entire metal portcullis and lock were electrified. *Clever*, he thought to himself. That part hadn't been mentioned in the catalog. Maybe Perfectus had ordered it custom made.

Wisps of smoke hung in the air. George sat up slowly, body aching, eyes squinting. On his knees, he searched for the tool. It had been flung from his hand during his flight through the air. His hands brushed against its metal handle. Grateful, he snatched up the tool.

A quick examination showed it wasn't destroyed or even damaged. Their motto really was true: "Built to take a beating and keep on defeating!" Good thing, too, because he needed it for his next plan.

He pushed the stethoscope tool back in its compartment for now. Twisting the tool slightly, he pulled out a set of wires and then carefully attached one to the floorboard before easing the other onto one of the metal bars of the door lock. As soon as both wires were in position, a giant spark arced between them. He wrinkled his nose against the scent of scorched plastic, but he smiled in satisfaction. The electricity portion of the lock had been short-circuited.

He felt like kissing the Tool for All Occasions. He'd

have to tell Sam—if he ever got the chance—that it was worth every penny just for the Short-Circuit Tool alone! George pushed the singed and melted wires back into the main compartment of the tool, making a mental promise to fix them later. He pulled back out the amplification device and set it against the lock without hesitation.

It was an old-fashioned spin lock, a good choice against most modern villains, who preferred breaking codes digitally. But George had been working hard to escape C Roster. He had mastered everything they'd offered in class.

He listened carefully as he spun the dial. The clicks of the lock's interior whispered its secrets to him. *Click.*

He stopped and spun the lock the other way. *Click.*

Back the other way. *Click.*

The lock sprang free.

George barely restrained himself from shouting with victory as the portcullis slid away from the door. He did a small shuffle-dance step for a second before the reality of the situation came crashing down on his head again. This was no class exercise. Every trial he passed just got him closer to his own defeat.

He sighed, terribly saddened by the thought. If only they hadn't stuck him in C Roster! He'd have passed this job up if he had even been B Roster. Well, too late to turn back now.

Putting the tool back in his belt, he pulled out his ray gun again. He wished he had thought to upgrade the handle to sweat-absorbent material.

George knew he couldn't kick down a door. He jiggled the handle, but it was locked, of course. Trying to pick the lock would require setting down his gun. He chewed on a fingernail, gazing down the hall. What if someone came up here? Well, it wasn't like he was going to really surprise Perfectus. The superhero's hearing was so good, he had to have heard the boom of the electric shock. The fact that he hadn't come out of the door made George wonder if Captain Perfectus was even home.

One way to find out. George banged on the door before he could chicken out. He lifted his ray gun so he could sight down the barrel. No scope on this model, since it hadn't been designed to fire at the distance it would now.

"Who'izts?" a garbled voice rumbled through the door. A heavy, shambling gait grew louder and louder.

George shivered, wondering if he had gotten this all wrong. Was he about to face something worse than a superhero? Sam's warning came back to him. Had Tuttle set him up? George lowered his gun slightly, uncertain, and then it was too late.

The door opened. Captain Perfectus glared out at him.

At least George *thought* it was Captain Perfectus. The man was certainly tall enough. The square, cleft chin looked right, though George had never seen three-day stubble on the captain's face. In pictures, the grinning superhero's skin was baby-smooth. His eyes always sparkled.

The eyes on *this* man were the same deep topaz George remembered from the many magazine articles, but these were… tired. Tired and empty. George's own eyes widened. His hand loosened on the gun.

Captain Perfectus looked right at him. George imagined what the man saw: a short, skinny villain who had clearly come to take him out.

The superhero sighed and shrugged. "You might as well come inside and have some orange juice before you shoot me. You know what they say about breakfast being the most important meal of the day."

Then he walked away, leaving the door wide-open behind him.

CHAPTER 16

THE BATTLE?

"THIS MUST BE a trap," George muttered. Why else lure him in? But... "Wait, did you say orange juice?"

George had always wanted to try orange juice, but it was, naturally, strictly forbidden for all villains, forever. And of course, Perfectus might be using the juice to knock George out.

George wasn't sure he cared.

Perfectus answered, "Sure, why not? One orange juice coming up."

George followed Perfectus into his suite. The luxurious apartment left George gaping.

"Holy Toledo," he said under his breath.

Perfectus remarked, "Spoken like a superhero, not a villain."

Great, George even sounded like a goody two-shoes to the biggest goody two-shoes on the planet.

Perfectus moved into the living room, not seeming to expect a response. Everything was so surreal.

Was he, George Pruwell, actually standing in Captain Perfectus's home? George spun around, taking in the entire room. It was a treasure chest: fancy furniture with leather and rich fabrics, important-looking paintings on the walls, jewel-encrusted awards on every shelf. A goldmine. He wondered if the Academy knew how much Perfectus was worth, considering this was his private residence.

Captain Perfectus snapped George out of his revelry with the sound of liquid gurgling. The giant superhero stood by a little refrigerator, pouring two glasses of orange juice.

"Come in. Sit down," Perfectus said flatly, setting one glass on the table with a clink. "I like the flames, by the way. Very dire-looking," he added, without even a smirk.

Guzzling the juice in one swallow, Perfectus flopped down on the leather sofa, grabbed the remote, and flipped through several channels before arriving at a nature channel. A lion was about to pounce on a gazelle.

This wasn't going at all like George had expected. He froze, wondering if the TV show held some hidden message, but Perfectus's head lolled on the couch. He wasn't even watching.

George kept his gaze away from the screen and lowered himself to the edge of a leather chair. He reached for the glass of juice on the table. Hesitating only a second, he wrapped his hand around it, even though it would be hard to fire his ray gun one-handed.

Perfectus drank a whole glass already, George reminded himself. It was probably safe. Still, it would be smarter to not drink it. But he could smell it now, the tangy, fruity sweetness of the juice. It brought to mind the prunes from breakfast. Deciding that if he was going to go down, he might as well do it with an excellent beverage in his stomach, George lifted the glass and took his first sip.

Oh, heaven! Holy mackerel! Nothing had ever tasted this good before in his life. Forget the bitter coffee. Forget the tasteless tea. If being an RPC meant he could drink this golden nectar of the gods every morning, he might not feel so bad about stumbling out of his family's footsteps. George's smile went from ear to ear. Before he knew it, not a drop of juice remained. He smacked his lips with gusto.

Captain Perfectus eyed him. "I assume you're here to attack me, seeing as you have a ray gun, a couple of grenades, and some special gadgets that look top-level?"

George felt the blush race across his cheeks. "Uh, yes, sir, sorry, sir," he stammered. *Back to the Duck Villain, then.*

Captain Perfectus grunted. "And what's in it for you? Besides the fame of defeating *me*, naturally?" His first few words were spoken with a hint of his usual commanding voice before quickly fading back to the same listless tone he'd been using since he opened the door.

"Does it matter?" George asked, far too embarrassed to explain to the most powerful superhero in existence about being a C Roster villain-in-training in need of a promotion. He wouldn't explain *that* to Captain Perfectus for all the orange juice in the world.

Perfectus sighed again—a long, loud sigh that slid the TV back two feet. George sat up straighter in his seat.

Perfectus finally answered, "No. It doesn't matter. Nothing matters."

"That doesn't sound very superhero-y of you," George said without thinking.

Captain Perfectus snorted, causing his juice glass to fly across the table from the explosion of air. "Superhero. Bah!" He slapped a blue couch cushion, which burst in a puff of feathers. Shaking off the feathers, Perfectus jumped up and began pacing. Small cracks spiderwebbed across the tile where he strode in increasing anger.

Well, that explains the hotel manager's desperate suggestion to tiptoe, thought George, ogling the damage with wide eyes. Captain Perfectus's pace picked up.

George kicked himself for saying anything. He'd have to work on keeping his mouth shut. He didn't think he was up to defeating *any* superhero, much less an upset one he was beginning to feel sorry for. Captain Perfectus was clearly having a very bad day.

Perfectus's hands clutched the sides of his head, and he started to tear at his thick black hair. He cried, "I'm no superhero! It's all a fluke!"

George raised his eyebrows and slid slowly off the seat, leaving his ray gun behind. He really didn't want to attack the poor guy now, but he didn't know what to do. None of the books gave instructions on what to do when a superhero had a breakdown. Did they have safe treatment places for people strong enough to bend solid steel bars?

If George told the Academy he couldn't do the job because of pity, he'd be stuck on C Roster forever or even be booted out. They were evil villains. Why should they care about this deranged man who was now talking to himself as he paced through the roomy penthouse suite, a blur of blue and black? But the thing was, for whatever strange reasons, George *did* care. *Dang it!*

Perfectus's muttering floated by in fits and snatches. He didn't even seem to notice that he was talking to no one but himself now.

George realized he needed to ask someone for help. This was out of his league. Maybe Tuttle would have some ideas; he'd been helpful before. But first, though, George had to calm down a very upset, possibly dangerous superhero.

CHAPTER 17

THE SUPER-BIG PROBLEM

IF PERFECTUS KEPT up this pacing, he'd wear a hole right through the floor. He really needed to stop. George realized this was sort of like soothing Alex during one of his snits. George figured he might as well use his hard-won comforting skills now to maybe keep from crashing through the floor.

"So... Perfectus?" George aimed for casual coolness. "It seems as though you were willing to let me defeat you without a fight when you opened the door." He let the statement hang between them, a dead mouse offered to a large cat.

Perfectus froze. His hair stuck out all over the place, but otherwise, he looked like the stone version of himself that towered in City Park in honor of the time he'd stopped Lightning Man from electrocuting everyone in the Empire State Building.

With a frown, Perfectus looked down his aquiline nose at George. "Do you really think I'd air my private business to an unknown youth such as yourself? Why on earth would I do that?"

Good point. "Well, you're not happy, right?"

Perfectus gasped. "I am *Perfectus*. How can I be *unhappy*?"

George pointed to the cracks along the floor from the man's pacing. "I'm just guessing that a happy person doesn't destroy his own home."

Perfectus sat down in a sudden slump in his recliner, head back, one arm draped dramatically over his forehead. "I can't let anyone find out."

George thought for a moment and then replied, "Look, I'm eleven years old, wearing tights with flames. Who'd believe anything *I* said about *you*?"

Perfectus mulled this over and then sat up in the chair. He leaned forward, almost eagerly.

"What I am about to tell you must stay in this room," he whispered, his gaze darting all around the walls.

George nodded, keeping his face calm. Inside, hope surged through him. If he could get Captain Perfectus to talk about what was upsetting him, maybe they could make some progress. What if he could even get Perfectus to move out without fighting at all? Maybe George could survive this after all. And maybe the Academy would even let him move up from C Roster if he could get Perfectus out of the city, even if he didn't do it through a battle.

Don't smile, George warned himself. Looking too excited would shut Perfectus down.

"It's my Incapacitator[20]," Perfectus said. "I… broke it!" He covered his face with his hands and peered out from between two fingers.

George tilted his head to one side. "That's it?"

The words popped out before he could stop them.

"*That's it?*" thundered Captain Perfectus. The windows rattled in their panes.

George gulped.

Perfectus continued. "I *broke* my own *super-tool*, boy! Don't you know my *name?*"

Ahh. The realization hit George like a ray gun blast.

---

20   Incapacitator: "Owned by Captain Perfection: This gadget shoots tremendously strong metal bands—aka 'loops like lead'—to tie up his enemies after being soundly defeated by the Captain's super strength. It is the last super-tool many villains ever see before their jail terms begin." From *Tools and Gadgets* class textbook.

"Yes, you're Captain Perfectus. The man who never makes a single mistake."

The man crumpled in the chair. "Exactly. I could hire someone to fix my Incapacitator, but if word gets out that I actually made a mistake… it would be the end of everything Perfectus."

"How did it happen?" George really wanted to know.

Perfectus's perfect face flushed the perfect shade of red apples. "I sat on it." He looked at George defensively then hunched over. "Well, the game was on. The Mets were ahead by two in the last inning! What do you expect?"

Keeping a straight face was the hardest thing George had ever done. The effort was definitely worth a credit in Poker Face 201. "Can I see it?"

Perfectus drew out a jumbled pile of cords and plastic from under a pillow on the couch.

George picked through the parts of the gadget. "It's a mess."

"Yes, I know." Perfectus buried his face in his hands again.

"You can't fix it?" George asked, surprised.

Perfectus shook his head. "I'm not talented in that

way. It's not my gift. I'm super strong, can fly, and can sense citizens in distress, but I can't use a screwdriver."

This time, George *did* chuckle, a small sound, but instead of infuriating Perfectus, it seemed to relax him.

Perfectus said, "I realize it *is* probably unbelievable. However, mechanical skills are not required for a hero to be perfect. But not breaking your own super-tools… that's important."

George smiled. "Well, nobody's *actually* perfect, right?"

Perfectus looked taken aback. "What do you mean?" Indignation soaked every word. "This is the only problem I have ever created for myself since becoming a superhero!"

George shook his head. How could a grown-up superhero not get it? Clearly, no one was perfect—not Perfectus and certainly not George. George was so imperfect, he was wishing he could fix a superhero's super-tool.

It wouldn't be too hard to fix, George realized. But if he did, he was closing the door for sure on being A Roster. He couldn't very well be a top-notch villain *and* rearm the very superhero he'd come to defeat.

George looked back at the man, who was pacing

again. By this point, Perfectus's usually sleek hair looked like a terrified squirrel clinging to his head. George sighed and shrugged. Who was he kidding? He wasn't going to be able to defeat Perfectus, with or without his Incapacitator. Even if it were possible, George just felt too badly for the man.

That meant George was C Roster or nothing from here on out, anyway. Any kind of glorious career was pretty much over. He would fail this mission and fail as a decent villain. But if he took advantage of Perfectus right now, George would feel like he'd failed as a human being.

His mom and brother wouldn't agree, of course, but… George took a deep breath and admitted the truth to himself. He didn't even want to defeat Captain Perfectus.

He wanted to *help* him.

It felt revolutionary to admit without guilt. Okay, without much guilt.

"I can fix this," George offered. He looked up at the stunned sound Perfectus made.

A broad smile crossed the superhero's face.

An answering smile spread across George's. Not only did he want to help, George realized, but he wanted this to be something he could feel proud of.

Helping Elizabeth had felt good, at least until he'd gotten busted. Helping Sam find his way out of the maze had made George happy. Even helping his mom with the groceries had always been a nice moment for him, despite her frequent reminders to be more selfish. Most of the time, helping others meant hiding his efforts, but maybe it didn't have to be that way.

He and Daniel had helped the squirrels together back home. Daniel had clearly enjoyed it, without shame. Maybe George could feel that way too, starting right now.

The major shift in George's goal made his brain feel a little like it had just been turned inside out by a mad scientist. Still, his mood soared. Lightness bubbled in him, as if he'd been cut loose from an anvil dragging him down. His heart felt rock-steady instead of confused and fearful.

He, a villain-in-training, here on a mission to destroy Perfectus, would help the dude instead. Plus, he'd get his hands on some awesome super-tool tech, even if it *was* a superhero's.

Helping a superhero. George shook his head. Alex would kick him. Heck, Sam probably would too. But George was going to do it anyway. It was the right choice, at least for him. He sat down to examine the damage, with

Perfectus hovering over his shoulder.

George made small talk as he studied the problem of the Incapacitator, cracking his knuckles as he prepared to dive in. "You know, I bet not a lot of people realize how hard it is to be the biggest, strongest superhero around."

"Well, that's true. Sometimes I just want to order pizza and play some video games, you know? Maybe read a good book while sipping tea. Not go saving another bank employee from an armed robbery. But, well, that's my job, you know? And I'm good at it. Why, I remember this one time—"

George nodded now and then as Perfectus talked about his adventures over the years and paced across the beautiful floors of his living room, stopping only to see how the gadget was progressing. His steps, though, grew quieter through each story. He even shared some of the silly mistakes he'd made when he was a very young superhero-in-training, like the time he'd accidentally flown into the glass wall of a tall bank like a dumb pigeon.

In return, George told the story about how he'd once tried to spy on his big brother, only to end up with black circles all around his eyes from the ink Alex had put on George's binoculars. The half-fixed gadget got pushed to the side as the two continued to talk and laugh.

"I once ate a bowl of staples that a villain had hidden in my morning granola. It didn't hurt me, of course, but I was like a staple gun every time I sneezed for a month!"

"I tried to keep a pet dog once, but it ran away after it smelled our mother's greens-and-beans meatloaf."

"When I was twelve, my first superhero outfit had a giant P on it—why must they always have those things?—and so my classmates called me Captain Pee-Pee until I got too big to tease."

They howled. Finally, out of breath, Perfectus sat down in his recliner again but gazed at George with sudden worry.

"I've never told anyone these things," Perfectus admitted, as if suddenly realizing again that his audience was an eleven-year-old. "You came here to defeat me, not befriend me." He looked uncertain and a little bit angry.

George realized he was about to lose this new fragile friendship unless he did something, something important. Something as terrifying as attacking a superhero and as embarrassing as wearing flaming tights. He would have to be completely honest about his own many imperfections.

CHAPTER 18

THE TRUTH

GEORGE BEGAN TO speak. "You don't have to worry about me, sir. I'm at the Academy of Villainy and Wrongdoing, but I got stuck in C Roster. Do you know what that means?"

Captain Perfectus shook his head. George sighed. He really didn't want to think about it, but he imagined Perfectus was feeling pretty uncomfortable right now himself.

"It means that I'm lousy at villainy. It means that even though most of my family has been feared and respected villains, I'll be some stupid sidekick or the kind of joker that superheroes like you don't even bother to catch. They let Regular Public Citizens catch us. Or worse, we trap ourselves and do dumb things and get made fun of all the time. It's humiliating. That's why I took this job—I wanted out of C Roster. But now I'll be stuck there forever because I've failed."

Captain Perfectus gazed at George, eyes thoughtful. "Who says you must be a villain? Do they force you to stay in this school?"

George sat back, stomach roiling. "I-It-It's what I've always wanted."

Perfectus raised one perfect brow. George couldn't blame him. He surely didn't sound convincing about his dream of villainy when he was helping a superhero. He'd just never even considered a different life until this moment.

"Then why are you in the lowest level of the school?" came the assured voice of the good captain.

"I was too nice to people," George mumbled, beginning to think he liked Perfectus better when he was pulling his hair out.

The superhero looked scandalized. "They punished you for... *kindness*?"

Perfectus's indignation was soothing. George had thought it was unfair too. Okay, sure, they were villains, but even villains needed to have someone to trust, right? Didn't everyone need a friend? He'd tried to be cold and calculating like his brother, but it hadn't worked. George just couldn't be that person.

"I guess I don't have the right talent," George

admitted. "I'll never get my Distinguished Villain plaque."

He imagined his mother's horror at his words. He pictured his brother, standing tall and proud with his dark cape flying. At least Mom would have Alex to carry on the family tradition.

George's predicament was worse than just not wanting to hurt people or steal from them. He actually liked being kind and *helping* them. The Academy would never stand for that in one of their villains.

But would his family even accept him if he left villain life, or would they disown him? Saying he could come home was different than actually leaving villainy completely. He'd never known anything else.

Captain Perfectus was suddenly standing right beside George and clasped his shoulder. "You have been a friend to me. That is a talent more rare than anything else in this world."

George's eyes stung. *Oh no.* He couldn't tear up. He resolutely stared out the giant windows until the lump in his throat dissolved. His brain felt like it had been shaken and stirred.

"Thanks, Captain Perfectus." He looked over at the superhero, who smiled his traditional toothy grin despite the purplish smudges of exhaustion beneath his eyes.

"Hey, why don't you get some rest?" George offered. "I'll finish up your Incapacitator, and later, I can even show you some easy tricks to fixing it in case it ever happens again, if you want."

George liked having a practical problem to solve. Being helpful was even better.

"I confess that sleep would be nice," Perfectus admitted. He wandered into the bedroom and crawled onto the mattress, his feet sticking out past the end.

George felt strangely uplifted. If Perfectus could face his failures, then surely George could face his too.

The truth was that he really wasn't the kind of guy who belonged in A Roster. That thought rolled around in his mind. He wasn't cutthroat. He wasn't ruthless. He was... nice. Maybe he could finally be okay with that. Hopefully, his family could be, too.

He smiled at the sight of the giant Captain Perfectus snuggled under his covers like a little kid after a long day. George relaxed as he turned off the lights and quietly slipped out of the room. Deep satisfaction wrapped him like a blanket. He couldn't remember when he'd felt this good, actually. No fear, no guilt. Just enjoyment.

George returned to the Incapacitator and carefully reconnected parts. The borrowed Tool of All Occasions was very useful here, giving the screwdriver, the magnet, and electrical socket he needed to recharge the battery as he worked on the rest. Humming quietly to himself as he worked, he thought of nothing but each necessary step to rebuild the gadget.

When he was finished, he took a deep breath and realized that he could actually fill all of his lungs without effort. He yawned, his body fading toward sleep now that the adrenaline was wearing off.

But first, he had another decision to make. Perfectus was now a friend. Not only could he not try to defeat a friend, George also couldn't stand by and let him get attacked by the professionals coming later. The team was going to be big and bad enough to maybe really defeat even Captain Perfectus. The big man wasn't a threat to the school—he didn't even know where it was located! He had been too freaked out about his broken tool to even think straight lately.

George decided he'd call Tuttle tomorrow and tell the school that Perfectus was no threat at all right now.

Then George's phone rang.

CHAPTER 19

THE CALL

SITTING UP, HE grabbed it without checking caller ID. He didn't want the ring to wake Perfectus. George hoped maybe it would be Tuttle, but it wasn't the teacher who asked, "How're things going with Captain Perfectus?"

"Alexander the Terrible? Is that you?" Shock tingled along George's fingers.

"Who else would be calling to make sure you're still alive?" Alex replied.

Warmth surged through George. His brother had called to check on him. So villains weren't all bad. A broad smile lit up his face.

Alex continued. "I haven't seen any news about Perfectus's defeat, so I assume you haven't gotten to him yet. You only have one more day. Are you going to succeed? Because you are a Pruwell, you know. You *need* to succeed."

George rubbed his hand across his brow. This was

not a conversation for the phone. He couldn't say, *Gee, no, I actually gave him a hand instead. 'Cause turns out, I don't want to be a villain.* Not to his brother. Not like this.

George's mind raced through various possible responses until he finally said, "Uh, maybe. It's sort of uncertain right now. Actually, Perfectus's not... what I expected."

There. That was neutral, right?

"*What? You're there right now?*"

George flinched at the volume. He yanked the phone away from his ear and could still hear Alex.

"*What's going on, bro?*"

If Alex knew George had backed off from attacking Perfectus, he'd be all over the superhero himself. George couldn't allow that to happen. Then again... he could feel his brother's lucky coin still pressed against the bottom of his foot. Alex had believed in him.

Maybe George had misjudged Alex, who'd even called to make sure everything was okay. His brother was a smart guy, a graduate of the Academy. He knew what kinds of things the school would expect from whoever took this assignment. Maybe if George were vague enough, Alex could actually help. Gingerly, George put the phone back on his ear. "Well, yeah, I'm here, but things are... weird. I could use some advice."

"Shoot," said Alex, sounding eager instead of his usually cool self.

"Captain Perfectus isn't really"—he searched for the right words—"the kind of problem the school thought," George said.

"Oh?" Alex said.

"Yeah, and I don't think I can defeat him right now. I'm not sure what to tell the school. Do you have any ideas?"

There. That should do it.

"Give me a second," Alex replied. There was a long silence on the line. Then he continued. "Relax, little bro. I'll get on my cape tonight. I wish I could teleport[21], but you'll have to hang on a few hours. All you gotta do is keep him in that apartment overnight, and I'll be there to help you first thing in the morning."

---

21 Teleportation—*The Idiot's Guide to Careers in Villainy* says, "Despite the misinformation spread by old TV shows, individuals cannot teleport through hulking mechanical devices. Teleportation is limited to an extremely rare subset of Sorcery Villains. Well, them and those they choose to send... elsewhere... which is why it is wise to be very, very nice to them. See also: *Sorcerer Villains.*"

George blinked, wondering how he'd gone from asking Alex a simple question to his brother joining him. That would be an awful thing for everyone.

Quickly, George said, "Thank you so much, Alexander the Terrible, but really, you don't need to come. Could you just tell me the best way to call the school and ask them to call off the assignment?"

"No!" Alex shouted, making George jump. "No, no, I'll take care of the situation. Don't worry about a thing," he said, softer.

George began to explain one more time, but he was talking to a dial tone. He stared at the phone and chewed his lip, uncertain of what had just happened.

Then he realized he hadn't given his brother Perfectus's address anyway. His brother knew he was at Perfectus's place but didn't know where that was. Well, that was probably just as well. When Alex called back to get the address, George would just explain that he couldn't give away Perfectus's secret location.

George would still have to call Tuttle or someone at the Academy. Or maybe Perfectus would have a suggestion once he was better rested. Maybe George would have a brilliant idea during the night. Well, he'd worry about it in the morning.

He crashed on Perfectus's couch, only bothering to drop his utility belt on the floor and take off his shoes. Alex's lucky coin fell on the carpet. George set the quarter on the coffee table next to him. Patting it once, he said, "Sorry, Alex. I'm just not the villain you are. I don't think I want to be, either." Then he fell into a deep, dreamless sleep.

The knock on the door confused George at first. "Mom?" he called, but then he remembered he wasn't at home. He wasn't at the dorm, either, he realized, feeling the smooth, leather couch beneath his hands. He sat straight up. Memories crashed through him of yesterday's adventure.

He was really at Captain Perfectus's penthouse in the Plaza. They'd sort of become friends! George couldn't even find it in himself to be scared about what he'd tell the school or his family. For now, he felt too good to worry. There'd be time for that later.

The sun glowed across the cracked ivory tiling and plush blue area rug, letting him know that early morning had come and gone. It was probably close to lunchtime. His stomach grumbled at the thought.

Then the knock clattered again, and he jumped. His mind whirled and cleared. Someone was at the door. He hopped off the couch, peered through the peephole, and nearly fell over. It was Alex.

CHAPTER 20
THE REAL CONFRONTATION

GEORGE GASPED IN alarm and chewed on a ragged fingernail while he watched his brother through the peephole. Alex was tapping his foot now.

How had he known where to go? Well, Alex could do just about anything sneaky. But why show up now? Maybe he was just here to give some moral support? He had called to make sure George was okay, after all. But if not, this could be bad, bad, bad.

Alex knocked again. He would wake up Perfectus in a moment.

A sudden idea struck George like a bolt from Lightning Man. He'd convince Perfectus to move back to his secret stronghold, which had to be somewhere other than the Plaza. As long as Perfectus stayed away from the Academy, they would probably leave him alone. No villain would want to mess with a superhero like Perfectus if they didn't have to. George smiled, extremely pleased with his new plan.

George opened the door, deciding to quickly tell his brother that the mission was off, but Alex pushed past him before he could say one word.

Alex strode into the apartment, air swirling behind him, along with the length of his white cloak. He kicked the door closed and turned to George.

"Where's Perfectus?" Alex asked, without preamble.

George blinked at the harsh tone in his brother's voice and glanced nervously toward the farthest door in the room. "He's—He's still asleep in the bedroom."

Only then did Alex smile. "Fabulous."

He whirled off the floor-length cloak, letting it fall to the floor, and George's jaw dropped. His brother had a new costume.

"It's impressive, I know," Alex drawled.

A crisp white suit covered his muscled torso and long legs. A thin white tie peeked out from behind the buttoned-up jacket. His dark auburn hair, swept up and back, looked like a crown atop all of that white fabric.

"I wanted to look my best to meet the biggest, baddest superhero of the ages," Alex explained, straightening his tie in the reflection of the glass window.

"Oh, he's not big and bad, Alex. I told you; he's really a perfectly nice person and doesn't need—"

Alex held up a hand to command silence. He got it. Long-standing habits died hard. "He may have *you* convinced he is helpless, little brother, but those of us with more experience are not so easily hoodwinked."

Dread pooled in George's stomach. This was a terrible mistake. "No, you don't get it, Alex—"

"No, *you* don't get it, little brother. You think I've waited all these months since graduation just to fade into nothing and become a laughingstock because you trusted a superhero?"

Suspicion crawled along George's scalp, and he swallowed hard.

Alex stalked up to George and leaned down until they were nose to nose. "No way. Not when a perfect opportunity like this lands in my lap. You led me right to him, even as weak as you are." He jerked his chin at the coffee table. "Told you that was my lucky quarter."

The meaning behind his brother's words took George's breath away like a punch in the gut. "You put a tracer on me? With your special coin?"

Alex laughed, a mean laugh that George suspected no one had ever needed to teach him. "Of course I used it to locate you, down to the precise square foot you were standing in. I could have hacked the Department of Defense and dropped a bomb on the apartment from space, except even *I* don't want to blow up my own brother, as pathetic as you are. But I did come prepared for Perfectus."

Alex swept off his suit jacket. His favorite ray gun was at his hip. George knew that gun was a high-end model and could probably shoot a hole in the wall even without any tampering. It might be enough to defeat even the strongest superhero of the ages.

George's stomach cramped. "Well, you always did tell me to trust no one."

Alex sneered. "And you never did listen. *Tsk, tsk, tsk.* Too bad, little bro. This is really for your own good."

George tried to explain again. "Alex, there really isn't a problem. I figured it all out. And he was really nice to me—"

A strange glint flickered in his brother's eyes.

George fell silent and took a closer look at the older brother he'd feared and admired for so long. A Roster, computer hacker, bank robber. Their father's hope.

Their mother's pride. Alex's cheekbones had always been sharp, but now they slashed along his hollow cheeks like razor blades. His eyes were sunken. His skin looked pasty like old glue. Alex was wasting away without the spotlight. And nothing would get him back in the spotlight better than defeating Perfectus.

Even as the thought slid across George's mind, his stomach roiled. Alex swept through the living room, scoping out the place for escape routes. He ducked behind a few pieces of furniture to check for good cover during a ray gun fight.

"So you're really going to steal my assignment?" George whispered.

"It's not like you were going to succeed, anyway, so don't whine." Alex pulled out his gun. "Now, where's the bedroom?"

I've been duped by my own brother, George thought. Alex really was a very good villain, better than George had realized. But understanding didn't stop his heart from feeling like it had just gotten stabbed by a Model A167

Broadsword from Medieval Villain Wear[22]. Then a peaceful sort of numbness came over him.

As if his brain's censor had powered down, George's next words were out before he could stop them. "If this is what being a Pruwell A Roster villain means, betraying your own family and stealing their chances, well, I don't want it."

Alex stopped finally moving and looked right at George. "Are you really that naive?"

The words were soft. Alex tilted his head the tiniest fraction, puzzlement clear in his eyes. He really didn't understand.

Anger seeped through the numb spot over George's heart. "Sam wouldn't have stolen my assignment before I even had a chance to finish it. But you? Oh yeah, you would."

Alex shrugged, double-checking the charge on his gun. "Don't know who this Sam is, but someone's got

---

22   Medieval Villain Wear: From their website: "For those villains who love the past era of knights, dragons, and easy-to-steal princesses. We have an impressive array of swords, armor, tunics, boots, and potion bottles. Note: For dresses, with this era, you're stuck with long skirts that hamper fleeing a crime and bad hats that hamper looking good. We suggest you move beyond the glorious tradition of the past. See our Sister Shop: Future Fabulousness."

to be the best villain. Someone's got to stand up in Dad's place." He straightened up, gun held ready in a strong, two-handed grip. "No one expected you to get the job done right. At least I'm keeping it in the family."

Years of being called weak by Alex, years of trying so hard to be bad, years of failing miserably, all built up like a pressure bomb inside George. Fury rose suddenly, a tidal wave of rage, swamping the numb spot, drowning him. Now he was ready to explode.

But he retained enough self-control to know that if he attacked his brother, he'd lose. His brother would defeat him and then quite possibly Perfectus, without mussing his carefully combed hair.

No, George wouldn't stop anything by attacking. He eyed the ray gun and made a split-second decision.

CHAPTER 21

THE GAMBLE

GEORGE HUNG HIS head, faking shame. Lowering his voice, he said, "Fine, you go ahead. You're right. You should do this for our family. I'm not strong enough. But, Alexander the Terrible, I need to warn you that Perfectus is even stronger than we were led to believe. He sleeps now just through that door, but I don't think your gun is strong enough to stop him. You'll only get one shot. Let me help you make it count."

"How?" Alex said, darkly suspicious.

"I learned a great trick at the Academy to make a ray gun twice as powerful. I can fix it in no time. I've got the tools right here." He pointed to the Tool of All Trades and silently thanked Sam for giving it to him. George didn't actually need the tool for this job, but his brother was always impressed by fancy appearances.

Alex sneered. "You always were puttering about

like a common RPC mechanic," he said. "Go ahead, but make it fast."

George did make it fast. He laid the ray gun on the table, thinking back to the first day of tryouts. His brother wasn't even watching, so confident in George's willingness to do whatever Alex said, just like always. Instead, he stood gazing out through the windows, craning his neck to look up at the neighboring skyscrapers.

George unscrewed the handle's end. Fear fluttered in his throat, but he swallowed hard and reached inside with his two smallest fingers to grasp the Light Containment Device. He quickly slipped it out of the gun and snapped the handle back together. The gun still made the charging sound from the battery pack, but now there was nothing to focus the light. It couldn't light a match now. George hid a smile as he slipped the LCD into his pocket. "It's ready, Alexander the Terrible."

Alex spun around, making his hair flare dramatically. He was definitely a great poster boy for Evil Villains. He stalked to the table and swept up his gun. "Thanks, bro."

"George."

"What?" Alex furrowed his brow.

"My name is George, not 'bro.'"

Alex glared and then he snorted. "Whatever... *bro*."

George allowed one cold smile to cross his face, the closest to a smirk he'd ever come. He moved to the far end of the room and got ready to duck behind the couch when everything went down.

His heart still ached a bit for Alex and probably always would, but George couldn't bow down to his brother anymore. It was time to do what was right.

"Captain Perfectus, watch out!" George shouted. A roar on the other side of the door confirmed Perfectus was awake. George knew the hero's superhearing would have already told him someone else was in the apartment besides George. Now Perfectus should know it was an enemy.

Alex shot George a look of panicked disbelief but stayed his course, running to the bedroom door and preparing to kick it open. Perfectus suddenly stood in the doorway, broad shoulders filling up the entire rectangle. Alex's gaze traveled up the length of him and stopped when he met Perfectus's fiery eyes.

Alex visibly gulped, but then he threw his head back, hair curling darkly against the white collar of his jacket.

"Say goodbye, Captain Perfectus!" Alex shouted and squeezed the trigger before the superhero could move.

Nothing happened.

Silence filled the apartment as Alex squeezed the trigger again and again. All the color ran out of his face until he was as pale as his suit. "Bro, you didn't!"

George ran to the rebuilt Incapacitator, snatched it up, and smiled. "Yes, bro. I did. Captain Perfectus—catch!"

The thin, silver stick flew through the air. George ducked down again as Captain Perfectus wrapped one giant arm around Alex and caught the tool with the other.

The sounds of scuffling were drowned out by a large, zapping crash.

"That'll hold you. You villains always underestimate people."

George peeked over the couch to see Perfectus tucking the tool back into his belt.

He smiled at George. "Call the police. They'll take care of him."

George looked at his brother struggling uselessly against the silver binding coils from the Incapacitator. The ropes were made of a special steel cord. Almost nothing could cut through them. George squirmed a bit as he watched Alex's face turn deep scarlet with anger and humiliation.

"Captain Perfectus, please let him go," George heard himself saying. Was he being foolish? Well, maybe, but he just couldn't send his own brother to prison.

Perfectus goggled in astonishment. George hadn't known that a superhero could look so goofy, actually. Running a hand through his hair, Perfectus sagged against the wall—the plaster groaned—and his eyes practically popped out of their sockets. "But he is a villain! He attacked me in my own home!"

"I know," George said sadly, pressing a fist against his chest. "But he's also my family."

Alex was already crying and promising to never use a ray gun again, which of course was a total lie.

"He'll probably walk and not get any real time in jail since he was using an inoperable gun," Perfectus responded. "Funny that the gun didn't have the LCD in it."

He gave a long look at George, lips twitching suspiciously. George grinned in response.

Perfectus shook his head. "I would do almost anything to repay the great favor you have shown me, but I cannot willingly set a villain free, even such a young one as this. It goes against everything I am," he explained. "*I* cannot." He raised an eyebrow and then rolled his eyes toward the floor, as if he were waiting for George to catch on to something.

George looked down at the ground, wondering what Perfectus was hinting at. It wasn't like George could do anything to help Alex. It was too late to help his brother.

Tears unexpectedly swam in George's eyes. He blinked hard, and a glimmer in his peripheral vision made him look closer at the floor. Christina's knife, still tucked in his tool belt on the floor by the couch! A plan sprang into his mind.

CHAPTER 22

THE OATH

GEORGE SAID, "PERFECTUS, could you please, uh, go downstairs and quietly ask for a policeman, just one, to come up here? I don't want a lot of media to see my brother."

The giant man nodded. "Of course."

Perfectus slipped out the door as quietly as a shadow, giving a quick wink.

As soon as he was gone, George grabbed the tool belt and rushed to his brother's side. He pulled out Christina's knife and pushed the button. The knife flicked out so fast, it made a hissing sound.

Alex's eyes went rounder than his tracking-device quarters. "Are you going to *kill* me?" he squeaked, a high-pitched sound George had never heard from his brother before.

"Don't be dumb," George replied, shocking Alex out of his tears and shocking himself while he was at it. Standing up to his big, bad brother felt better than expected. Way better.

I should have done this years ago, George thought, chuckling to himself.

"I'm glad you find this so funny." Alex scowled.

For the first time, that look didn't set George's knees to knocking. Instead, he met his brother's gaze straight on. "If I let you go, will you swear The Oath on your honor as an official villain of the Academy that you will fly out of here and never return to harm Perfectus?"

"I don't think you have the ability to let me go."

"You'll never know if you don't swear."

Alex was silent.

"Fine, have it your way," George said. "Maybe you and Dad can finally get some quality time." He smacked the knife against his palm—*smack, smack*—casually walking away.

"All right!" Alex snapped. "I swear The Oath to leave and never return to harm Perfectus, on my honor as an official villain of the Academy."

George let out a sigh of relief. Alex would never betray The Oath. Being a respected Academy villain was the only thing that mattered to him.

Happily, George jumped over to his brother's side and then slid Christina's knife under the metal coils, cutting upward. The metal cut like cooked spaghetti. In seconds, the coils fell to the floor with a clank. Amazing.

Alex flexed his hands and stomped his feet a few times to get the feeling back in them. He looked at his little brother. "That was a smooth trick with the gun… George."

That was all Alex said. And even though it had been reluctantly gritted out between his teeth, George treasured the message hidden among his brother's sparse, strained words.

Footsteps sounded from the hall, growing louder every second. Alex grabbed his cape and whirled it over his shoulders while snapping the collar around his neck in one smooth move. He really did have some prime cape skills. With two giant leaps, Alex was at the patio doors, and one more step sent him soaring into the air.

George watched him go, feeling as light as the clouds that soon hid his brother from view.

When Captain Perfectus arrived with the police officer, he met George's eyes. George nodded. Perfectus nodded back and said in a calm voice, "Oh no. My goodness. The prisoner must have escaped. George, are you okay?"

George replied, "I am, yes, Captain Perfectus. He

just escaped. I'm so glad you're here, in case he comes back for me."

Perfectus sent the disappointed police officer back downstairs and looked hard at George.

"I'm sorry I cut through your Wonder Cords, sir," George confessed immediately.

Perfectus waved his hand. "I use *Recycling is Super* to recycle my used ropes. No worries." He paused for a moment before continuing. "I understand the importance of family, George, even though I don't have one myself. I fear, though, that you have set him free only to have to face him again one day, perhaps without someone like me to help."

A chill raced through George, but he shook it off. "I appreciate your concern, sir, but he's my brother. I'll take my chances with him. Thanks for everything, Captain Perfectus."

George meant every word.

Perfectus still looked at him with concern. "But what will you do now? Though it will be clear you did not defeat me, we could always say you enacted a successful getaway." His topaz eyes twinkled. "After a huge and hard-fought battle of course, from which I narrowly escaped with my life."

George laughed before he grew serious again. "I

doubt anyone would believe that. Besides, I'm not sure I should go back to the Academy even if they'd take me. I'm not very good at being a villain."

"And I'm not very good at fixing things," Perfectus responded. "Would you like to stay with me, then? I could use a sidekick."

George thought about it. For a long minute, his mind was filled with glorious images of flying next to Perfectus, of beating back bandits and saving the human race in one fell swoop.

But then he remembered Sam and Christina and Elizabeth. His mom, his dad, his brother: all villains, all people he cared for.

No, the Academy was not the place for him, but neither was life with a superhero.

"Thanks anyway, Captain Perfectus. I think I want to do something else. But I need you to do something for me first." His thoughts raced ahead as he figured out what this decision meant for his life.

"Anything, young friend."

George smiled. "I need you to take a vacation. A long one. And move back into your secret stronghold when you're done."

Perfectus's eyebrows shot up. "Why will I be doing this thing? What will the world do without Captain Perfectus?"

"Trust me. You need a rest. You won't get one staying here," George replied, thinking of the professional team hired by the Academy that would soon arrive on the scene.

"And this will help you?"

"More than you know, Captain Perfectus. Trust me."

That evening, George reported to Tuttle in person. George hadn't wanted to give his bad news over the phone. "Perfectus is gone but not defeated."

Tuttle shook his head. "I know. Social media showed him sunbathing in Rio. He even had one of those little umbrella drinks. But since he's not near the school anymore, the contract on him has been dropped."

George smothered a smile. His newest friend had looked really happy.

"Sir, with all respect, I would like to withdraw from the Academy of Villainy and Wrongdoing. I am not cut out for this life, no matter how awesomely villainous my family is."

Tuttle wrinkled his brow. "What will you do then?"

George felt the grin try to spread across his face again, and this time, he let it. He could smile as much as he wanted now. "What do most eleven-year-olds do in this country, sir? Go to school, make friends, have fun. That's what I'm going to do too. I can enroll as a sixth grader in public school back home right away."

Tuttle gasped in horror. "Go to a school for Regular Public Citizens? Do you think you'll actually like it?"

George laughed. "We'll see, won't we?"

An hour later, George hopped in a taxi. He waved at everyone who'd come to see him off: Sam, Christine, Elizabeth, Derek, even Chancellor Tuttle. George smiled, though his eyes burned a bit. He knew he wasn't really saying goodbye, just 'see you later,' but still... he'd miss these people. His friends.

At least he definitely planned on visiting. Sam already had some plans for more New York sightseeing. And the next time they talked, George would be able to give them all up-close-and-personal intel on what life was really like on the other side as an RPC.

As Sam had said, "You've got so many things you

could teach those regular kids. It could be a ton of fun—they'll never know what hit them!"

George slept through the flight and took a taxi home without calling first. He wanted to surprise his mother. The house looked exactly the same as when he had left, down to his *Evil at Work* sign on his door. But George had changed so much.

His mother's reaction to his choice was much better than expected. She gave him a tight hug and, after checking for any injuries, said, "It's been so *quiet* here with you gone, and Alex has just moved out to his own lair and, well, I'm glad you're home, honey."

Then she fixed him a roasted radish, even though he didn't have to eat that stuff anymore. She agreed to take him to enroll at Crestley Middle School first thing Monday morning.

He'd be entering a month late into their school year, but George was still excited. For the first time, his whole life was before him, blank for whatever he wanted to put in there. He had no idea what he wanted to do for his future career, but whatever he chose would fit who he really was. Choosing his own path was scary but definitely cool.

He wasn't sure what regular school might hold for

him, but he'd already gotten accepted into the Academy of Villainy and Wrongdoing, made friends with people trained to not make friends, helped the biggest superhero of all time, and stood up to his brother. How hard could life be as a regular sixth grader?

Captain Perfectus sent a shiny plaque that proclaimed in scrolling letters, *The Worst Villain Ever*. On the back, he had written, 'Thank you for being the best friend a superhero could ask for. —Perfectus.'

That very night, George took down the old sign on his door and replaced it with his new plaque. He thought back to how he'd once sworn to be known as the worst villain of their time. He would never have a Distinguished Villain plaque, but this one was better. Just looking at it made George smile. The Worst Villain Ever. A title he could be really proud of.

ACKNOWLEDGEMENTS

In 2010, I was in the middle of drafting *Fairy Keeper* when an idea popped in my head about a sweet kid in a villain family, trying to make them proud. I set *Fairy Keeper* aside and wrote *The Worst Villain Ever*. I thought it would be my first published book. Instead, it is my 8th!

Maybe it's because of this long history that George has such a special place in my heart. *Worst Villain* helped me get my first book contract in 2014... for a different book. Then it was almost published in 2018 with a small press that closed its doors just prior, and then another publisher didn't quite work out, either. Finally, Snowy Wings Publishing gave George a home!

Several editors have given excellent feedback over the years. Thanks go to editors Krystal Dehaba, Madeline Smoot, and Amy McNulty. Author Bev Katz Rosenbaum also critiqued this story years ago, along with editor Amy Lin at Editomato in 2011. I received helpful feedback from several online contests too. Red Adept Editing provided excellent proofreading services! And huge thanks to Snowy Wings Publishing, with extra applause to Lyssa Chiavari!

This book wouldn't be the same without my writing friends and critique partners, especially my earliest readers and CPs: Carol, Lara, Stacy, Jeannine, Ann, and Mary. Special thanks to Garrett, my first young reader of this story. My former SCBWI critique group overseas and my current fabulous critique group have offered amazing support. Thank you!

The delightful cover is thanks to Qamber Kids, especially Najla Qamber, Nada Qamber, Jenn Silverwood, and illustrator Oh Lenic, who delivered the cover of my dreams. The interior formatting (with those tricky footnotes!) was done beautifully by Nada Qamber at Qamber Designs.

To my family—I love you and appreciate your steady support over the years!

And finally, to those reading—thank you for sharing your time with me and my characters! I'm grateful every day for you all.

—Amy

ABOUT THE AUTHOR

AMY writes magical escapes for young readers and the young at heart. She is the author of the World of Aluvia series, The Secret Psychic series, and the Wish & Wander series, beginning with Paris on Repeat. She is also a former reading teacher and school librarian. As a military kid, she moved eight times before she was eighteen, so she feels especially fortunate to be married to her high school sweetheart. Together they're raising two daughters in San Antonio.

You can find Amy online at amybearce.com.

OTHER BOOKS BY AMY BEARCE

Wish & Wander

Paris on Repeat

Rome Reframed

The Secret Psychics

Shortcuts

Detours

The World of Aluvia

Fairy Keeper

Mer-Charmer

Dragon Redeemer

OTHER BOOKS FROM SNOWY WINGS PUBLISHING

SUPERDREW AND THE SECRETS OF DONHIL CORP, BY BJ PIERSON

Thirteen-year-old Drew Stirling, tinkerer and computer geek, may need braces to walk, but the add-ons and customizations he's made have turned them into SuperDrew braces: stronger, faster, and full of more gadgets than he could ever need. When Drew is turned down for an internship at the ultra-mega-cool Donhil Corporation, he's willing to do anything to prove he's good enough to join the world's top inventors—including sneaking into their regional office to get a scoop into their newest products. But instead of insight into their uber-healthy fast food and ultra-fast custom transportation, Drew finds out that maybe Donhil Corp is more like a supervillain than a superhero.

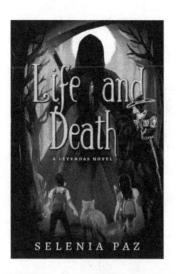

LIFE AND DEATH (LEYENDAS, BOOK ONE)
BY SELENIA PAZ

When Natalia's younger brother disappears while on a visit to Mexico, Natalia is certain that La Llorona, the mythical Weeping Woman, has taken him. Her friend Miguel agrees to accompany her back to Mexico in the hopes that it will help him deal with the recent death of his grandfather. But as they embark on a journey to search for the creature that has taken Natalia's brother, it becomes apparent that the spirits Miguel had brushed aside as mere legend are very real... and they have a dark connection to his family.

www.snowywingspublishing.com

CPSIA information can be obtained
at www.ICGtesting.com
Printed in the USA
LVHW110725041122
732323LV00003B/81

9 781952 667794